Praise For Mark Sadler and Touch of Death

"Mark Sadler writes of despair and violence with sizable narrative talents."

—*New York Times*

"Mark Sadler knows both the topside and underside of the New York scene. He writes about both with intelligently controlled ferocity and speed."

—*Ross Macdonald*

"Will intrigue and surprise even the most jaded mystery buffs."

—*Santa Barbara Magazine*

"His style has a distinctive resonance all its own."

—*San Francisco Chronicle*

Touch of
Death

MARK SADLER

BERKLEY BOOKS, NEW YORK

TOUCH OF DEATH

A Berkley Book / published by arrangement with
the author

PRINTING HISTORY
Berkley edition / December 1988

ISBN: 0-425-11261-6

A BERKLEY BOOK ® TM 757,375
Berkley Books are published by The Berkley Publishing Group,
200 Madison Avenue, New York, NY 10016.
The name "BERKLEY" and the "B" logo
are trademarks belonging to Berkley Publishing Corporation.

PRINTED IN THE UNITED STATES OF AMERICA

10 9 8 7 6 5 4 3 2 1

To Jennifer, Roberto
and everyone at
The Cloak & Dagger

One

THE OTHER TIME they took John Thayer to the hospital he had been beaten almost to death. This time it was only a worn-out gallbladder, but for me the result was the same. Someone had to mind the whole store alone. With Dick Delaney on a tough case out in Los Angeles I was it, and that meant Maureen would have to be alone on location the whole month or more. It wasn't going to do much for our marital bliss.

"You married an actress. You let her become big box office in Hollywood," Thayer tells me every chance he gets. "A woman's place is in the home."

He's our senior partner, and work is all he really gives a damn about. Paying work. My private life is of no interest to him unless it gets in the way of a case. He likes to work alone, keeps his cases to himself, and if he hadn't gone into the hospital that week, I'd never have met Sarah Jurgens or heard about the boy.

"He could be anywhere from ten to fourteen, Mr. Shaw. He's small, thin and pasty faced, and I've never seen him up close."

Sarah Jurgens still held Thayer's card tight in her hand as she sat at my desk. Thayer, Shaw and Delaney—

Security and Investigations: New York . . . Los Angeles. I'm Paul Shaw. Thayer and I hold down the New York office, Dick Delaney handles Los Angeles. The L.A. office is in Hollywood on Wilshire Boulevard, and our New York office is on Madison Avenue. "No Tenth Avenue or Broadway hustle," Thayer never stops instructing. "No more hooch, heaters and 'stash the boodle, doll.' Today we're businessmen, and we need a successful business image."

So we have two private offices in a bank building and a large and impressive reception room. The furniture is Danish modern, and the secretaries are Finnish blond. Clients who enter stiff and wary, expecting to smell sweat and bourbon, relax when they see an office the same as all the other offices where they have spent their lives.

Sarah Jurgens might not have entered our offices at all— with relief or anything else—if I hadn't come back from lunch in time to find her walking the corridor outside, pacing and twisting Thayer's card the way she still twisted the card across my desk.

"What do you want us to do about the boy?" I asked.

"I want to know who he is, what he wants."

"What do you think he wants?"

"I don't know." She looked at something over my shoulder. The buildings outside my windows and the distant East River. "Three times he's come to the house. That is, three times when I was there. They go into Matt's study. No introduction, no explanation. All three times Matt has come out—" she searched for the word she wanted, the office silent except for the typewriter out in the reception room "—disturbed . . . shaken. Yes, shaken."

"You know the boy's name?"

She shook her head. "I want to know what he's doing to my husband, Mr. Shaw."

What she really wanted to know was what her husband was doing. A natural blond, her hair was a shade too long for her thirty-five-plus years, but she had the figure of a woman a good many years younger. She wore a slim black-and-white-check tweed suit and a black turtleneck blouse, soft black leather boots up to the skirt and an elegant mass of bracelets and gold chains. She worked hard on looking good for someone. Even harder than I'd first thought because as I looked closer at her tight face I realized that she had to be over forty.

"An address?" I said. "House, hotel, apartment?"

"Nothing."

It meant a stakeout at her house to pick the boy up and tail him. On top of our base per diem fee we have fixed charges for stakeouts and tails and other time-consuming routines, plus expenses and overtime. We usually quote for a seven-hour day, but I didn't get to quote anything to Sarah Jurgens.

Out in the reception room a man's voice shouted, *"I want to see my wife!"*

"Please, sir, Mr. Shaw is busy. You can wait—"

Sarah Jurgens stood up. "It's Matt!"

"How did he know you were here?"

"I don't know."

"Sarah! Where the devil are you?"

"You want him to come in?"

She nodded. "Yes, all right."

I walked to the door and opened it. A short man in a brown suit was nose to nose with my blond Finn, Ellie. Small and skinny. A thin neck and short gray hair. He looked like a man who didn't care what he ate or how he dressed. The brown suit, white shirt and brown tie were rumpled, the cordovan half boots scuffed. His narrow face had beard shadow. A gray man in a brown suit. Except for his eyes. They were large and bright and looking at me.

"Where's my wife!"

Sarah Jurgens faced her husband. His manner changed the moment he saw her, as if that was all he had really wanted. He touched her arm.

"A private detective, Sarah? Is something wrong?"

I closed the office door. "How did you know your wife was here, Mr. Jurgens?"

"Mrs. Wright told me she'd gone to New York. I found the address on the telephone pad."

"Mrs. Wright?"

"Our cleaning woman," Sarah Jurgens said. "I forgot I wrote down your address."

"Why?" Matthew Jurgens said. "What *is* wrong?"

"That boy, that's what's wrong! Who is he?"

"Boy?"

"What does he want? You go into your study. You close the door. You—"

"Good God, it's just business. Work I'm doing at home for a new client. The boy brings it."

His voice had been puzzled, his eyes confused, from the moment he started talking to her. Now he sounded relieved, as if it was all right now that he knew. I watched them, and I knew he was lying. The whole thing was an act. He had known what was bothering his wife before he ever came to my office. But was the act for her benefit or mine?

"I'm sorry, I should have told you," he said to her, "but this new client is difficult. I've been worried. Look, what if we go out to dinner tonight and talk it all over? I've been too damned busy lately, I know that."

"Well. . . ." She wanted to believe him.

"I'll pay Shaw, of course."

"My partner would insist," I said.

"I'm sorry, Mr. Shaw," Sarah Jurgens said. "I've wasted your time."

"In my work," I said, "it's better when it turns out that there isn't any job after all."

Matthew Jurgens paid me our fifty-dollar-minimum consultation fee and took her out of the office on their way to a dinner that would cost him a lot more than fifty dollars. I wondered if it was going to be worth it to him. He was lying, but how much and why? Whatever, they seemed to be going to work it out without me, and with Thayer in the hospital I had other work to do. I almost forgot about Sarah Jurgens and the boy.

Two

THE TELEPHONE RANG at four minutes after midnight a week later. She was hysterical.

"He's hurt! Oh, he's bleeding! Hurry! Oh, please—"

I tried to calm her. "All right. What happened?"

"Help me! Hurry, please! Oh, the terrible violence! He's hurt, bleeding! Hurry!"

I managed to calm her enough to get their address. It was in Douglaston. Damn! It showed she wasn't thinking. Even past midnight on a weekday I couldn't get there in under half an hour.

"Mrs. Jurgens? Now listen—"

"Why do you keep talking? Hurry!"

"Sarah! Listen to me! Call your police station. Tell them to send the paramedic team. Do it now. I'll be there as soon as I can. The paramedics. Now."

Maureen, my wife, is a successful actress. Very successful—New York and Hollywood. We live in a penthouse on Central Park South with a view all the way uptown. A view as dark now as the city ever got, the park black through an autumn drizzle. Dressed, I holstered my working pistol, a light six-shot Colt Agent with a two-inch barrel, and went down to the deserted and echoing garage.

In the small red Ferrari Maureen had bought me last Christmas I drove out into the night city.

The streets were empty in slackening October rain. I took the Midtown Tunnel and the Long Island Expressway across Queens. Traffic had been held down by the rain, but even at one o'clock on a Wednesday morning it surged around me with hazy headlights and the hiss of tires. Giant cities never sleep. Someone or something is always moving among the lights and shadows.

The North Shore suburbs on the Nassau County line are bedroom communities of the middle affluent, built around the bays and harbors of Long Island Sound. Douglaston is the last of them inside city limits. The streets were almost dry; the rain had stopped here earlier than in the city. The Jurgens house was a on quiet street a few blocks north of Northern Boulevard.

A two-story white colonial with blue trim, it had tall oaks and maples, ivy and climbing wisteria. An older house on a small lot, separated from its neighbors only by the trees and a different atmosphere. On a street with yards full of footballs, toys and broken wagons, the Jurgens house had a neat, empty lawn and a well-kept silence. The best house on a quiet street that wasn't quiet now.

As I parked, I saw that the house was a blaze of light. A paramedic van, two patrol cars, a Medical Examiner's wagon and some detectives' cars were all parked in front. The neighbors were out in coats and nightgowns. I showed my license to the patrolman guarding the driveway. He went in to check with his lieutenant. The lieutenant cleared me and I went inside.

There was an entry hall with a large living room off to the left, a formal dining room to the right and a wide center stairway going up to the second floor. Sarah Jurgens sat on the stairs. She heard me come in and looked up. Her eyes were flat and unblinking.

"Too late," she said.

"Where is he?"

"Too late. He's dead."

"What happened, Sarah?"

"Matt's dead."

"How did it happen?"

"He was dead when they got here."

I went into the living room. Behind me she continued to talk to no one in particular. Across the large comfortable living room with its fireplace and marble mantel there was another short hall and a door to what had once been a side porch. I had to show my credentials again at this door. To a detective who called into the room that had been made out of the porch, "Hey, Lieutenant, we got a P.I. out here. Says the wife hired him."

"Christ! He had to be riding the medic truck. Run him in here."

The room was a man's study—large desk, typewriter, files, leather couch and armchairs, and a wall of books. A quick glance showed most of the books to be on advertising, public relations and journalistic reference. A private sanctum with a color television, a stereo and tape deck, and a stocked liquor cabinet. The man who'd had me sent in was tall and heavy, in his early fifties, with thick black hair and a battered face. He looked like an old heavyweight boxer who could never get a suit to fit him after he retired. He was surrounded in the small study by his detectives, a lab crew and two paramedics, and the M.E.'s physician working over the body of Matt Jurgens.

"Lieutenant Guevara, precinct squad," he said.

"Paul Shaw, Thayer, Shaw and Delaney, and we don't have to ride medic trucks."

"Lucky you. John Thayer? Lawyer type, small mustache and rimless glasses, skates pretty thin?"

"I'm not a lawyer. I don't skate thin."

"Then how'd you get on this so fast?"

I told him. He was interested in the scene in my office a week ago. Even more in her call to me tonight.

"She wasn't thinking too good," he said. "Terrible violence? That's what she said?"

"Yes."

"And he was alive when she called you?"

"That's how it sounded. He was dead when you all arrived?"

Guevara nodded, and thought. He turned to the medical men.

"When did he die? As close as you can."

The two paramedics didn't even look up. They weren't going to make any guesses that could end up later in court.

The M.E.'s man said, "Anywhere from five minutes to two hours before you all got here. Say ten-thirty at the earliest."

It meant that Matt Jurgens could have died twenty minutes after Sarah had called me, an hour and a half before or anywhere in between.

"You got anything else I should know?" Guevara asked.

"Not yet."

"Okay. Stay out of the way."

He was giving me a break, so I blended into the wallpaper. The study was a mess, torn up by a fight or a search. Jurgens lay on his back to the right of the desk as if he'd been working and had come around the desk to meet his killer. He had been stabbed twice in the chest, once each in the left arm and shoulder. I saw no other marks or bruises. In shirt-sleeves, the right sleeve torn. I spoke to one of the lab men.

"Anything under his nails? Blood, skin, hair?"

"Clean as a baby."

With no bruises it meant no fight. A search then. For what? The drawers and files had been pulled out and dumped, the desk chair broken, tables knocked over, and a lamp smashed. The desk top was untouched. The knife lay on it, bloody and tagged for evidence. An antique dagger for dueling, twelve inches long. A fingerprint man dusted it.

"Anything?" I asked.

"His and hers and a lot of smudges."

"It was his own knife?"

"Got it on a trip, she says. Souvenir."

The M.E. had taken the body out, the paramedics had gone, and the lab team was going when two detectives brought Sarah Jurgens into the study. Lieutenant Guevara sat down facing her. She still wore only her nightgown and bathrobe, her youthful body looking slimmer than ever under the folds of loose cloth. A contrast to the face that now showed her forty-plus years against the long blond hair. She was a good-looking woman but tired now, lost.

"Tell it to me again, Mrs. Jurgens," Guevara said.

She nodded. "I was asleep. Upstairs in our bedroom. It's over the garage, I don't know why I didn't hear him come home." Her voice alternately flat and breathless, monotonous and eager.

"Your husband was often out at night?"

"Almost never. I don't know where he was. Some business. He never told me much about his business. Perhaps I didn't ask."

"What was his business?" Guevara asked.

"Advertising and public relations. His own agency. It's so much more work to have your own agency. You're at everyone's beck and call, there's so much traveling. I never did like it. Now . . ."

She let the word hang. Lieutenant Guevara waited, but it went on hanging—whatever "now" was going to mean to her.

"You were asleep," Guevara prompted. "You didn't hear him come home."

"No," she said. "I'd gone to bed early. I don't like to be alone. I woke up to this terrible shouting and crashing and banging. An awful row."

"Shouting and banging at the same time?" Guevara wanted to know. "Or at different times, maybe?"

Her tired eyes were vague, disoriented. "I'm not really sure. I seem to remember hearing most of it all at once, but I have the feeling that I didn't, that I was awake at different times. Half awake and half asleep. I thought Matt was in bed. I told him to go down and stop whoever was making all that noise. By the time I realized I was alone, it was quiet in the house. I went downstairs. I found the front door open. I found a window open in the living room. I found Matt . . . bleeding . . . bleeding. . . ."

"And called Shaw?" Guevara said.

She stared at a wall. "I needed help. Mr. Shaw had been going to help. I couldn't seem to think. I'm not sure I can, even now. I had to call someone."

"The shouting, was it anyone you knew?"

"When it was quiet, before I came down, I realized that it had been Matt. Matt and some other voice."

"You didn't recognize the other voice."

"No. There could even have been more than one."

"Was it a man or a woman?"

"I couldn't tell. I heard the voice or voices, but I understood nothing, could identify nothing."

"Who would have wanted to kill him, Mrs. Jurgens?"

"No one."

"No enemies?"

"I don't think so. Not even many friends. Matt wasn't the gregarious type. There was really only his work."

"Any problems at work? Trouble in his agency? With partners, clients, maybe competitors?"

She shook her head. "I told you he never said much about his business. He did say that he had a difficult new client. Mr. Shaw heard that, but he never told me the name of the client." She shook her head again, almost sadly.

"Competitors?" Guevara said. "Partners?"

"Agencies don't really compete, it doesn't pay." Her voice was suddenly impatient with Guevara's ignorance of reality. "Matt started the agency with his brother and sister. Estelle just put up money, and Bill died a few years ago. Bill was a bachelor, left his shares equally to Matt and Estelle, so Matt had the controlling interest in the agency."

"Was anything stolen tonight?"

"I don't think so, not in the house. Anything valuable is in our little safe, and it wasn't touched. I can't say about this study, I have no idea what Matt might have had in here."

"All right, Mrs. Jurgens. We'll watch the house, and if you hear anything or think of anything that might help us track the killer, let us know."

She nodded. The police started to wrap it all up. I went into the living room and sat down in a corner.

* * *

Sarah Jurgens walked through the silent house turning out the lights. In the living room I watched her from the shadows of my corner.

"Okay," I said. "let's talk."

"About what?" she said. She turned out another lamp, moved on to the next.

"What you didn't tell the police—the boy."

She turned out all the lights except the ceiling fixture in the entry hall and sat down across the room from me. Her face was half in shadow, the shape of her slim body visible under the robe and gown.

"Why didn't you tell them?" I said.

In the half-light from the entry hall her face seemed suddenly no longer so tired, the vague, lost look gone. There was a hard set to her jaw now, anger in her large eyes, determination on her full lips.

"I want to know more before I do, Mr. Shaw. I want to know a lot more. About the boy and about Matt. Perhaps I won't have to tell them at all."

"Matt didn't tell you all about the boy when he took you to dinner last week?"

"No more than he told me in your office," she said. "He talked a great deal, but it never turned out to be anything but a small business problem, and the boy was just a messenger. He was sorry he'd been so busy, away so much lately, but he didn't really tell me anything. Just a nice expensive dinner."

"You don't think the boy was a business problem?"

"Not a small one anyway," she said in the half-light. "Matt went to a lot of effort to find me in your office. I wanted to believe him. He seemed concerned about me, was paying attention to me. Perhaps that was all I wanted after all."

"Didn't he usually pay attention to you?"

"When he was at home he did."

"You said it was unusual for him to be out at night."

"It was, but it wasn't unusual for him to be away. A day, two days. A week, a month. Business trips, short and long."

"But you don't believe the boy was business."

"Not the agency business."

"What makes you so sure?"

"Matt was never that concerned about business. He knew his work, the agency was successful, he always said no business was worth an ulcer. He was worried by that boy and business problems never worried him."

"You think he was in trouble, you want me to find out what it was."

She turned her head to look toward the study where Matt Jurgens had died. I saw her face in profile like a silhouette. The normally soft curves and pouting mouth had hardened into firm, almost harsh, angles.

"I want to know who that boy is, what he was doing here. I want to know what he meant to Matt."

"Could the second voice you heard have been the boy?"

"I'm not sure. Perhaps."

She still sat with her profile turned toward her husband's study, the shadows marking her face with strong lines and angles that seemed at odds with the soft lips and small aquiline nose. Still a good-looking woman; at half her age she would have been stunning. An interesting woman of sharp contrasts. The slim, well-cared-for body, the soft face that showed its true age only in wrinkles around the eyes and then the unexpected harshness suddenly in the face.

"Two hundred a day," I said, "plus expenses."

She shrugged. "I've got plenty of money now."

I stood up. "Get me the address of his agency and a retainer check. I'll be back."

I went outside into the dark silence of predawn. The rain had stopped. The temperature was falling fast, heralding the coming winter. A brick path went around the house and across the front lawn to the street. An old path, muddy in many places under the trees. Neither the police nor I had used the path, and I went slowly down it examining the patches of mud. Twice I saw the print of a canvas running shoe. The left foot both times, small, and going toward the house.

There were no other footprints on the path. As I turned to go back to the house, I saw the car. A red Olds Cutlass with twin tail pipes. It wasn't a street where cars parked overnight at the curb, and as I watched, it pulled away and vanished. Had the driver pulled away because he saw me looking at him, or was it just some lost traveler who had stopped to look at a map?

On the path that circled the house I stopped at the open living-room window. Plants and earth had been trampled under the open window. There were no recognizable prints, only the muddy depressions where someone had stood for some time, depressions partly washed away and full of water. Some of the trampled, but unbroken, plants were already rising again from the mud.

Back in the house I heard Sarah Jurgens somewhere upstairs. I shut the living-room window on my way into the study. A table and the carpet under it showed no damage from the earlier heavy rain. In the study I closed the door behind me. The police had put it back in order as they examined and photographed everything that had been moved, touched or searched. I went over the whole room again.

Nothing was obviously missing. Whatever the reason for the search had been, with Jurgens dead we weren't going to find out in the study. The books and magazines

on the shelves all seemed old and unused, the shelves were
dusty, and all the papers in the files were dated far back.
Matt Jurgens may have worked at home years ago, but it
seemed that what Sarah had said about recent years was
true. There was nothing else of interest to me except a
desk drawer full of matchbooks from bars, restaurants, go-
go joints, hotels, coffeehouses and bistros from cities all
over the country. There were five on top, all partly used,
from a place called El Jazz Latino with an address in the
East Village.

I took one of the El Jazz Latino matchbooks, went out
into the living room. The small piece of cardboard would
have been hidden by the shadow of the couch leg except
for the angle of light from the hall into the dark living
room. A stiff piece of beige cardboard with numbers and
a badly printed name and legend: Al's Loans—We Buy
Anything. The address was on the Bowery.

Sarah Jurgens had come downstairs to the kitchen. She
had made a pot of coffee, sat now at a table of dark polished wood. The single light above the table made her eyes
shine. She had taken off her robe, and her youthful body
showed naked underneath the nightgown. She poured a
cup of coffee for me. I sat down. She smiled at me, and
it wasn't the light over the table that made her eyes shine.
Large eyes, bright and distant as if seeing something she
wanted a long way off.

I said, "He had a lot of matchbooks in his desk."

"He collected them."

I laid the El Jazz Latino cover on the table. She glanced
at it, touched it and shook her head.

"Any reason for him to be in the East Village area?"

"No."

I placed the ticket from Al's Loans beside the matchbook. She touched the ticket, frowned at it.

"What is it?"

"A pawn ticket. From the Bowery."

"Pawn ticket?" Not many people under sixty in Douglaston would recognize a pawn ticket. Something from an alien world.

"Who's been in the house recently besides the boy?"

"No one."

"No visitors for either you or Matt?"

"Matt went on a trip last week, got back Sunday. I've been here alone."

I asked the questions. She answered. But I knew that talk wasn't what she wanted tonight. I've seen it before, the shock and the loss, the need to feel alive in the face of death, the need to feel that tomorrow will come. I knew what she wanted, she was an exciting woman, and Maureen somewhere in Arizona wasn't the only one alone because Thayer had gone to the hospital. But I would pass this time. It wouldn't be me in the bed with her, it would be the shade of her dead husband. A desperate subconscious attempt to bring him back to life.

I told her to take a pill and get some sleep. I would call her later. I left her sitting at the kitchen table, drinking her coffee and watching me with those distant eyes.

Outside in the gray dawn I spotted the red Olds Cutlass again, parked far up the street this time. This wasn't some lost traveler looking for the Throgs Neck Bridge. Half-hidden by two old oaks and a maple that grew almost in the street, the red car was out of sight of the patrol car parked in the driveway of the Jurgens house. The cop in the car was probably asleep anyway.

Someone leaned against one of the old oaks a few yards from the red Olds. A small person wearing a black beret and a raincoat. It could be a man or a woman. Both hands in the pockets of the raincoat, silent and unmoving under the old oak. A warning, telling me I had been spotted, was known. I wanted to grab him or her. To maybe shake something out of him. But all I could do was stand in front of the house and stare back across the dark distance. At my first step toward the silent watcher all he had to do was stroll to the Olds and drive away before I could get near.

So I got into my Ferrari and drove toward the parkway. In the rearview mirror I watched the shadowy figure and the Olds as long as I could. They didn't move. It wasn't only me they were concerned with. The police would protect Sarah Jurgens, but who and what were they?

I had been ready to collapse into bed, start work tomorrow, but the red Oldsmobile and its silent watcher had my juices going again. A good breakfast, a lot of coffee, and get to work. It beat an empty bed anyway.

Three

I LIKE BREAKFAST made by a good short-order cook in a busy diner. I don't get it often. Maureen is someone who thinks by the book: you can't have a side dish of asparagus with a bowl of lamb stew, no matter how much you like asparagus, and good food comes from good restaurants. But Maureen was away, so I stopped for eggs, bacon, homefries and toast in an all-night diner on Amsterdam Avenue in the Eighties. I drank coffee until eight-thirty, then drove on downtown to the address Sarah had given me for Matt Jurgens's agency.

A four-story brownstone on West Twenty-second just off Sixth Avenue, the front steps removed long ago, it had a chased brass nameplate: Jurgens Associates: Advertising and Public Relations. (That "Sixth" Avenue is an affectation, what old Manhattanites still insist on calling the renamed Avenue Of The Americas, and Manhattan is my home. Where I learned I couldn't act, met Maureen and decided that being a detective helped me to feel I was doing something useful.) I parked in a garage three blocks away and walked back.

The agency receptionist smiled up from behind an inlaid and gilded antique desk in a reception room that occupied most of the street floor and looked like the salon of an *ancien régime* French count. With her black hair and the high Indian cheekbones many Puerto Ricans have, the girl's smile was almost as dazzling as the room. I gave her our card.

"Mrs. Jurgens sent—" I began.

She hesitated—private detectives weren't in her office manual—but she decided quickly who should handle me, whatever I wanted.

"I'm sorry, sir, Mr. Jurgens hasn't arrived yet. If you'd care to wait, I'm sure he won't be long."

The office staff hadn't heard. Which meant that the police had not been here yet, and Sarah Jurgens hadn't called with the news. She was probably finally sleeping. I didn't know what the cops were doing. I was about to tell the girl that Mr. Jurgens would be a very long time coming in and why, but I didn't get the chance. A large, handsome, dark-haired man with heavy brows over pale brown eyes came in like a tropical storm on its way to becoming a hurricane. The receptionist looked surprised, glanced at her watch almost by reflex. The big man saw it, and he didn't like it much.

"Early to be clock-watching, isn't it, Carmen?"

The receptionist wasn't bothered by the rebuke or even concerned.

"I thought I was seein' things, Mr. Jellicoe. Why, even Mr. Jurgens isn't in yet. Hey, maybe you could help this gentleman? He wanted to see Mr. Jurgens."

She was saying right to his face that he never got to work on time, and that he carried no weight with her. I expected him to explode. He didn't. He only stared at her as if he planned to remember her and her remark. Then he almost shook himself and looked toward me as if he had suddenly heard what she said.

"For Mr. Jurgens?"

"He's a private detective," the receptionist said.

The big man, Jellicoe, stopped looking at me. "He'll just have to wait. Let Harry Glanz talk to him when he comes in. If anyone wants me, I'll be in my uncle's office."

"I *told* you. Mr. Jurgens isn't in," the receptionist said.

She took a hell of a lot of liberty with someone higher in the company than she was. Maybe she had protection or knew that the big man carried no muscle at all. A nephew of Matt Jurgens. Sarah had said that the brother had never married, and the big man's name wasn't Jurgens, so he had to be the sister's son.

I looked closer at him. At least six-foot-four and a lean two hundred and ten, he was the picture of a young, athletic Ivy League type with little taste for contact sport. The tennis or ski team, and probably still club champion somewhere. Regular, beautifully normal features, handsome as all his friends would be handsome, as if they had all worn braces not only on their teeth but on their whole faces. His wife would be lean and precisely dressed in a sporty manner, except at evening parties when she would wear formal clothes about ten years behind the international set. His children would be incredibly healthy looking. If he had children. The seventies had not been an era of children in the suburbs, more a time of self-development. A Brooks Brothers gray glen plaid with cordovan brogues, striped blue shirt and rep tie. All as it should be, yet not quite, a hair askew. His pale brown eyes, were not content—even overbearingly confident—as they should have been. The eyes were restless and resentful, almost sullen, as if the whole picture wasn't his own idea—shaped, smoothed and even dressed by someone else—and it wasn't paying off exactly the way he had expected.

Sarah Jurgens hadn't mentioned that Jellicoe worked at the agency. Maybe Sarah hadn't considered him important, and he didn't seem to be, at least not to the receptionist who appeared very sure of herself. I would have said she was right until Jellicoe suddenly put both hands flat on the antique desk and leaned toward her with a wolfish smile and more than a hint of violence in his pale eyes.

"I don't care what you told me, Carmen. I don't care what you or anyone tells me. Mr. Jurgens—"

The woman who closed the outside door delicately and then walked regally toward Jellicoe and the sneering receptionist silenced whatever Jellicoe had been going to say about Matt Jurgens. She was an angular woman in her late forties who walked like a dowager queen, erect and haughty. Except that she wasn't quite old enough looking to be a dowager, her short black hair only shot with gray, her sharp face not yet heavily lined. Too hard for a queen consort. More like a reigning queen, her chin high to show that she was both indomitable and privileged. A modern queen in a gray cashmere coat over a navy blue wool dress, slit to show her good legs in spike-heel shoes.

"Mother?" Jellicoe said. "Did I forget something?"

The receptionist smiled reluctantly.

"Mr. Jurgens isn't in yet, Mrs. Jellicoe." Her voice was more polite than it had been for Jellicoe, if only a shade.

Estelle Jellicoe advanced toward her son, but I had the feeling it was me she was really seeing, and that she knew exactly who and what I was.

"Peter," she said. "Your Uncle Matt won't be in today or any day. He's dead."

Peter Jellicoe said nothing. He stood there at the reception desk, big and handsome, and watched his mother. It was the receptionist who half screamed, her hand over her mouth.

"Mr. Jurgens! No, you got something wrong. You—"

"Murdered," Estelle Jellicoe said, still looking only at her son. "Last night in his house. Sarah called me this morning, Peter, after you'd left for the office. She said she'd hired a private detective to find out who did it."

The receptionist stared at me. "You knew! You knew Mr. Jurgens was dead, and you didn't say—"

"I was going to," I said. "No one gave me the chance."

"A knife," Estelle Jellicoe said. "He was stabbed, Peter."

"I don't believe it," Peter Jellicoe said at last. "Not Uncle Matt."

"Sometime around midnight last night," his mother went on. "Sarah called the police and the paramedics, but it was too late."

"Terrible." Peter Jellicoe shook his head. "A terrible thing. Poor Aunt Sarah. Maybe you should go and stay with her awhile? I'd send Lee, but the kids are sick. And the agency! What do we do? Matt was almost the whole company. The driving force anyway."

"Still," Estelle Jellicoe said, "he had been slacking off, letting the rest of you do more work."

In the plush reception room I listened to them, and there was something forced about it all, hollow. An act, like Matt Jurgens that first day? Estelle Jellicoe hadn't really come to tell Peter that Jurgens was dead, but to tell him that I was on the case? Had Peter already known his uncle was dead? Had both of them? Was that why he had come to work early, had been hurrying to Matt Jurgens's office, had suddenly become tough with the receptionist? I could be wrong, but Peter Jellicoe had come in like a man in a hurry, and he hadn't said anything when she had told him Jurgens was dead until after she'd mentioned me.

"We'll all go on, Peter," Estelle Jellicoe said. "Someone else must take the responsibility of running the agency."

"And soon," Peter said. "We've got the Christmas campaigns coming up. I'll get the section heads and the lawyers to meet fast. Aunt Sarah should be there, but if she's not up to it now, I can handle her interests as well as yours, mother."

"She should appreciate that," Estelle Jellicoe said. "You need her power of attorney and her proxies."

They sounded like a pair of ghouls carving up a still-warm corpse. An elation in both their voices they couldn't quite hide for all their show of stunned shock and loss. Almost bursting with anticipation. I could see that the receptionist had the same picture. There was a hard look in her dark eyes, a grim set to her jaw that said she knew that if they were in, she was probably out. And the eyes said the hell with them. If they were in, she wanted out.

"I'll talk to Sarah at once," Estelle Jellicoe said.

"And I'll call the meeting in Matt's office," Peter said.

It was going to be a fast, hard shot at taking over. A naked grab. At the least, a pair of ghouls. And at the most?

"I want to look at Matt Jurgens's office," I said. "Mrs. Jurgens gave me a free hand."

"I don't care what—" Peter began, angry.

"Of course, Mr. Shaw," his mother said.

"Well," Peter said, "all right then. Of course."

He had a wife and children, but it was clear who ran him.

"Can I ask where you two were around midnight last night?"

"I was at home, Mr. Shaw," Estelle Jellicoe said.

"With your son and his family?"

"My son doesn't live with me," she said, testy. "He's a grown man. I was at home alone."

"You live alone?"

"I have a housekeeper. My husband departed some time ago. Not as finally as Matt but nearly as abruptly. I am quite happily divorced. The housekeeper was out last night."

In short, she had no alibi.

"Were you at home, too?" I asked Peter Jellicoe.

"No, I was out."

"Where?"

"In New York. Later I dropped in on mother."

"Doing what here in town?"

"As it happens, I had a meeting with a client, but there was a misunderstanding. He didn't realize it was the night and never showed up."

Meaning that if I talked to the client about the alleged meeting, he would say he hadn't known there was one. I didn't bother to ask the name of the client.

"When did you get to your mother's?"

"I don't know exactly. Probably about twelve-thirty."

"How probably?"

"Almost exactly," Estelle Jellicoe said. "Do you suspect one of us of killing my brother, Mr. Shaw?"

"I don't suspect anyone yet. Where do the two of you live?"

"In Great Neck," Peter Jellicoe said.

"Both of us," Estelle said.

Great Neck is only two stops past Douglaston on the Long Island Railroad, a matter of minutes by car. Neither of them had an alibi, and Peter had been in the area at the right time.

"Who was the new client giving Matt Jurgens trouble? Making him work at home, sending messengers."

They seemed genuinely confused, looked at each other.

"I never heard of any client giving him trouble," Peter said. "In fact, we don't have any new clients."

"None?"

He shook his head. "All with us at least three years, most even longer. New business has been zero for some time."

"Because Matt stopped pushing, stopped tending to business," Estelle Jellicoe said.

"What was he tending to?" I asked.

"I don't know," she said.

"Wasn't he on the road a lot? On business?"

"Too much," Peter Jellicoe said. "From the start the agency has been too much a one-man show. After Uncle Bill died, it got worse, and now we could be in trouble."

It sounded like a speech he'd had ready for some time and was now producing for his shot at convincing everyone he was the man to step into Matt Jurgens's shoes. For his and his mother's grab at control. Chance? Luck? Or had one of them sort of helped chance along a little? One of them or both of them.

At the rear of the second floor of the brownstone, the office where Matt Jurgens had worked was quiet and shadowed. I searched it carefully, but there wasn't much to search. Furnished in the same elegant taste and manner as the reception room below, it seemed somehow bare and Spartan. Except for the desk, everything in the room was unused. The couches and chairs looked as if no one had ever sat in them. There was nothing in the gilded chest of drawers, and the inlaid French cabinets were empty.

There was only the desk to search, and everything on it or in it was strictly business and no help to me that I could see—except another drawer of matchbooks, some again from El Jazz Latino and some from other Village and East Village clubs. That was all, except for the contents of the wastebasket—mostly discarded envelopes, drafts of business letters full of positive public relations, and crumpled memo pages with scrawled notes on them: "Ted Garou . . . New Orleans . . . 66; Sarah . . . Thursday; Pick up tickets . . . Rudy; Ray Johnson . . . Chicago . . . 440."

I sat behind the cluttered desk for some time. Matt Jurgens had not been a neat man, and the messy desk made the rest of the office seem even more untouched. I had a vision of him alone behind the desk in the center of the unused room like someone on an island. He had worked here, but not much else. Peter Jellicoe might complain that Matt Jurgens had been too much a one-man show, but from the aura of his office the agency had been just a business to Jurgens, only a part of his life and maybe not even the most important part. Somehow I knew, sensed, as I sat in his bare and silent office, that there had been something more in his life. I wondered what.

When I came out of the office the employees were all gathered in small groups in the doorways of their offices, and there was a loud hum of voices from up on the third floor where the clerical services of the agency were. No one spoke to me, and I didn't see Peter or Estelle Jellicoe. I went down to the reception room. The Jellicoes weren't there, either, but the receptionist was. She stood behind her ornate antique desk clearing it out.

"Fired?" I asked.

"I'm not waitin' to find out," she said. "You think they maybe killed him?"

"Did they have a reason to kill him?"

"They both hated his guts. The little boy because uncle wouldn't give him any clout around here, an' because he's one hungry-for-power boy. The sister because big brother never let her nose into the business, an' because he wouldn't give the little boy the power.''

"You knew Matt Jurgens pretty well, Carmen?" I said. "It is Carmen, right?"

"It's Carmen," she said. "I knew Mr. Jurgens. He hired me. That's why I'm gettin' out. No one else around here would have hired me. I don't figure they'll keep me too long, you know?"

"Not even Sarah Jurgens?"

She laughed. "The 'Douglaston Duchess'? No way."

"Why did Matt Jurgens hire you?"

She closed the desk drawer and her bulging handbag. "Maybe I was a good receptionist."

She walked out without looking back. So did I.

Four

EL JAZZ LATINO was on St. Marks Place off First Avenue. Three steps down from the street and set back across a narrow stone terrace that had been under the outside stairs when the now renovated old-law tenement had been built. Before ten in the morning the street was busy, and so was a man with a mop inside the open door of the club.

"Closed, *amigo*, sorry."

I showed him my business card. "I'd like to talk to the manager and the bartenders."

"Nice address you got for a shamus," the mop man said. "Classy." He leaned on the mop, grinned. "Bartenders are all gettin' sleep or somethin'. Owner's inside. He's manager, bouncer, barkeep and you name it."

"He's my man then," I said. "Point him out."

"Just walk in an' follow anythin' that moves."

I saw the gray-haired older man across the vast room polishing glasses behind a long bar to the left. What had once been many small rooms had been converted into one large cavernous space that still had the vertical load-bearing beams cutting it up like the pillars of some temple. A temple of music, from the large bandstand at the far end with a set of old but sleek drums on it showing the initials "EG."

"Eddie Gallant?" I said to the man behind the bar.

"You know your jazz," he said, looked back toward the drums in the great silent room and then at me again. "Cop?"

He was short and broad, the caricature of a Mexican or older Puerto Rican, but the mandatory mustache was missing, he had no accent at all and his steady eyes were not those of a caricature. Eyes that looked me over and missed very little, and a thin mouth in a kind of perpetual small grin as if the world amused him.

"Private," I said. "It shows?"

"An Anglo in a Brooks suit in this place at ten on a Wednesday morning is looking for something."

"Other people come looking."

He smiled. "I'm clean with city hall, Albany and the Feds."

"I'm looking for answers about Matt Jurgens."

"To what questions?"

"You know Jurgens?"

"Yes, I know him."

"He came here a lot?"

He polished a glass. "Has something happened?"

"Why would he come down here? It's a long way from his office and in the wrong direction for his commute."

"You could ask him."

"Did he come in here alone? Or with someone?"

He bent to put the glass under the bar. When he straightened up, his face had changed. Nothing I could put into words, but he was a different man. I had made some mistake. Even his voice was different, part of the caricature now.

"Hey, maybe you be'er ask him, okay?"

"I can't," I said. "He was killed last night at his home."

"What you know? Hey, tha's too bad, *amigo.*"

"He was murdered," I said. "Who would want to kill him? Why?"

"You lemme know when you finds out, man."

"Look, I don't know what I said that got your back up, but I don't want to have to bring the cops down here."

"Muy bueno! You a nice guy, you know?"

"What was it?" I said. "Because I didn't say he was dead? Asked who he came in here with?"

He polished another glass, his long Castilian face impassive. *"Qué pasa?* I don' understand English so good."

"Did he ever come in with a boy?" I described the nameless boy as Sarah Jurgens had described him to me.

He shrugged. "Gringos, they all look the same, *sí?"*

I left him polishing his glasses in the vast morning silence of the catacomblike jazz club with its dimness and its pillars. I could have lost him because I didn't tell him what had happened to Matt Jurgens, or when I asked who Jurgens had come to the club with. Either or both. It made a difference. He could just have been angered by my holding out, or he could be protecting someone.

Skid rows are the same in all the cities of the world. No matter what the buildings look like or the clothes of the good citizens or the color of the forgotten and abandoned, the hopeless streets and crumbling faces are the same. The denizens shuffle along the bright or dark streets, unaware of the difference, oblivious to all but their purpose of the moment. They gather in doorways, on the street corners, in the garbage-strewn alleys, small groups around the same center—a bottle. They lie sleeping wherever they drop, derelict obstacles for the walking to step over. Or they limp slowly and alone, going nowhere at all, no purpose even of the moment for the more than sixty percent who are not drunks or vagrants—the old, the enfeebled, the solitary impoverished who can live nowhere else.

Al's Loans was a large pawnshop between a grimy flophouse hotel with boarded street-level windows and a stink I smelled a block away, and a liquor store with shelves full of endless bottles of dark and white port, cheap Tokay and even cheaper muscatel, its windows covered with paper signs that proclaimed bargain prices in enormous black letters—prices that would turn out to be only a little higher than on Park Avenue. (Any good businessman knows that you make more money from the poor than from the rich.) Across the street was a mission kitchen, the customers already lined up, the unfortunate who didn't even have a short dog of port, who stood with their hands in their pockets hunched over even in the October sun. Al had picked his location well, had them all zeroed in.

Inside, it was a prosperous-looking pawnshop with modern electronics behind the counters, old-fashioned wire cages in front of the counters and every conceivable item piled or hanging from floor to ceiling. There were binoculars, telescopes, cameras, musical instruments, jewelry, suits, sporting equipment, radios, television sets, medals, watches—trays and trays of watches behind the glass and wire. The pawned pasts of a million wandering souls. Al, too, knew how and where to make money.

"What you got?"

The man inside the wire cage looked like a gorilla smoking a cigar. Short black hair bristled from the top of his round head as he sat bent over some papers, talked without looking up. I pushed the pawn ticket through the cage opening. He didn't look at it.

"Sometime today, maybe?" I said.

He looked up, surly, and then stood up and took the cigar from his mouth. He almost saluted. I wasn't the type he usually got. Maybe he'd never seen a three-piece dark suit. He looked at the ticket.

"You wanna buy it back?"

"That's the idea," I agreed.

He lumbered off somewhere out of sight in the big store, and I watched the derelicts shuffling past the windows in the October morning light, framed by the shop's stacks and rows of shiny items they had turned their backs on long ago. The clerk came back with an expensive-looking bracelet and a puzzled expression.

"How much?" I said.

"Two hunnerd 'n fifty," he said, eyeing me, still puzzled.

The bracelet was probably worth at least a thousand dollars. Not what I would have expected to find in a skid-row pawnshop, and I hoped the clerk's puzzled expression meant what I thought it did.

"Not much for that bracelet," I said.

"Boss got a lot o' overhead."

"You remember who pawned it?"

Now he looked me up and down. He seemed disappointed in me. I'd failed him.

"Cop?"

"Private," I said. "That ticket turned up last night in the house of a murder victim. The bracelet could get awfully hot. Who pawned it?"

He didn't hesitate. Not in a murder case. I'd been right about the puzzled expression. He'd known I hadn't pawned the bracelet.

"A kid. I remember him pretty good 'cause I took one look 'n figured the bracelet got to be stolen. Only when I make him the offer anyway, he says it's lousy 'n he got to run home to his ma to find out if he can take it. I figure that's it. I ain't gonna see that kid again 'n good riddance.

So help me, he comes back and says okay he'll take the two-fifty. He ain't gone five minutes, you know? So I figures the bracelet ain't hot after all 'n gives him the cash.''

''You have a name and address?''

''Sure do.'' He lumbered off again. I waited, wondering if it could be this easy. He returned. ''Ted Garvey, 1480 East Second.''

''Thanks,'' I said.

''Hey! Don' you want the bracelet?''

''Keep it safe for the police.''

I retrieved the pawn ticket—I'd need something to hand the police when I finally told them—and walked north to Second Street and then east. And it wasn't going to be that easy. The address given by ''Ted Garvey'' was an empty store, stripped inside and boarded up.

Along the noontime street, women in housedresses watched me from steps and open windows. A phony address, yes, but the boy had to know the empty store to use the address, and the pawnshop clerk had said that the boy wasn't gone from the shop five minutes when he went to consult about the price offered. He had to live somewhere near. All I had to do was find where.

There was no way to go door to door on skid row. No one was going to tell me anything in the tenements, flophouses or hotels. Not the way I was dressed. Not asking questions like a detective. Being up all night was about to catch up on me anyway. I would drive back uptown to our penthouse, make a telephone call and go to bed. Sleep, wait for the night.

I stood in the silent shadows of the night alley. Small feet scurried among the shards of broken glass that littered the dark ground. The stink of garbage mingled with the hot stench of urine and the lingering odor of cheap sweet wine.

From time to time drunks shuffled through, their short dogs of wine clutched under their ragged coats or held in paper bags inside the pockets of their shirtless jackets.

I watched them from where I waited, hidden in a dark doorway recess. None of them gave the sign I was waiting for. None of them noticed me. I went on waiting, motionless. The drunks wouldn't notice me if I did a dance, but on skid row you never knew who else might be watching.

Two of the drunks didn't reach the far end of the alley. They swayed, collapsed against the wall, slumped to the dark ground. Down drunks, the target of the predators who prowled the streets and alleys of skid row. Today was the second "Mother's Day" of the month—one of the two days when the social security, veterans' pension and disability, and welfare checks are delivered. A good drunk roller or a lucky amateur can clear a thousand dollars on a good "Mother's Day," and the risk is minimal. Even if a down drunk rouses momentarily from his stupor to fight more for his short dog than any cash he has left, it is a feeble fight in a world of half consciousness, and a few kicks, a silent knife, will send him back to sleep sometimes permanently.

But it wasn't a quick silent jack roller who slipped into the dark alley next. Another drunk, another derelict, and not one of the fortunate with his precious short dog or even a real bottle. A slow-moving wraith in rags who checked the litter of bottles, the battered garbage cans, for some ray of hope and reached within a few feet of where I stood silent in the hidden doorway.

"You there, Shaw?"

His voice was not drunk.

"I'm here."

"I told you never roust me 'Mother's Day.' "

Not drunk, but nervous. Very nervous. He should have

drunk by now. He wasn't, and that showed how scared he was. His name was Freddie, better known as Writer, and I'd never met anyone who knew his last name. He was an alcoholic with no need to reform, a onetime author not good enough in his own eyes, a man who had lost his family in an air tragedy fifteen years ago. He had no need to live but couldn't die and made some of the money he needed for his bottles by finding out things I wanted to know anywhere south of Fourteenth Street. He once told me he would be as horrified to find out there was a God as to find out there wasn't, and he didn't like being a paid informer, but he needed his bottles.

"No choice," I said from the shadows. Neither of us moved. A hidden tableau, with me rigid in the shadows and him bent over and searching in the garbage can. "What do you have, Writer?"

"Word's around about a kid jack roller fits your boy. An amateur, working only the last couple of weeks. Lives at the Grace Hotel, a flop over on Clinton, with his mother."

"Got a name?"

"No, but something's funny. They're scared in the alleys. The kid scares them. They know he's rolling the alleys, but they don't want any part of stopping him, catching him. Something about him, some connection, scares them, and the word is out to look the other way. Stay away from the kid and do nothing."

"You don't know what it is?"

"Only that it's not the kid himself. Something else."

"That's it?"

"You have an address."

He has the best grammar of any informer I work with. I paid him his money. That is, I laid it on the ground inside a folded newspaper and pushed the paper out of the niche with my foot. He went on poking through the garbage until he "found" the newspaper. Then he slouched out of the silent alley toward his private Jerusalem to be born again in the peace of a bottle.

I gave him ten minutes, then eased out of the dark doorway and headed for Clinton Street.

Five

THE FIRST PIECES fitted at the Grace Hotel.

It was an ancient six-story firetrap with wire cages covering the windows on the first two floors, a rusted cast-iron marquee and a battered sign in blue-and-white glass. A pair of steps worn down so far they looked like bowls led into a narrow lobby with dirty walls, a dirtier white tile floor and a scarred and stained Victorian desk at the far end. An out-of-order sign hung on an open-cage elevator. The sign looked as if it had been there at least since World War II. Open stairs went up next to the elevator and vanished through a door on the second floor. There were wooden benches and a closed newsstand that probably hadn't been open since the headlines announcing the sinking of the *Maine* and the start of the Spanish-American War.

The desk clerk was a balding man with a young face and old eyes. Up close I saw he couldn't be more than twenty-five, prematurely bald, with nervous eyes and a flabby face that looked as if it never saw the light of day.

"Yes, sir?" He seemed as astonished to see a man in a suit with a vest and tie as the pawnshop man had been.

"I'm looking for a boy." I gave him the description

Sarah Jurgens had supplied. "He's supposed to be here with his mother."

"That's the Garou kid. Ted Garou."

And there it was, the first connection. To what I'd found on the crumpled memo sheet in the wastebasket in Matt Jurgens's office: Ted Garou . . . New Orleans . . . 66.

"How long has he lived here?"

"Mrs. Garou's been here about two weeks."

"Does she have a room number?"

"Sure, twenty-seven, but they're not home now."

I got a ten out of my pocket. "I'm going to sit over in a corner. When the boy comes in, give me the high sign."

He nodded, took the ten eagerly. Skid row was one of the few places in the country these days where a ten-dollar bill still had any weight. I found a spot on one of the hard wooden benches from which I could see the desk while staying hidden by the closed newsstand. I lit a cigarette, watched the clientele wander in and out. None of them looked as though they'd seen even a ten-dollar bill in months. Most of them were old, all of them were bent. Twisted in some way as if their bodies reflected their lives. The losers, bent by an indifferent world. Injured and abandoned and drifting here to be forgotten.

I saw the boy and the woman an hour or so later. I didn't need the nod of the clerk over the shoulder of the woman as they stopped at the desk for their room key. The boy was small, thin and pale with large luminous eyes that seemed to watch the world from a distance. A face like those of refugee children in old war photos, of a concentration-camp survivor. Eyes that looked at everything as if searching for something and not finding it.

The woman wasn't much taller than the boy, only a few inches at maybe five-foot-four, and had the same large eyes, but she was neither thin nor pale. She had a full female figure, well curved and padded in all the right places, and a pretty face with good color. She could be any age from twenty-eight to thirty-eight, but a tired walk, the discouragement in the lines of her body, made me lean toward the higher figure.

They went up the stairs and through the door to the second floor. I nodded to the clerk and followed them. It was an old hotel, numbered not by floor but in numerical order, and room 27 turned out to be the third floor. I came out of the stairwell as they reached the door of the room, stepped back into the shadows to wait until they went inside.

The woman opened the door, went in and screamed.

A hand reached out and dragged the boy inside.

A man's hand and arm. I saw a black-haired wrist, a heavy watch that looked expensive even in the dim corridor light and a brown suit sleeve. Then the door slammed shut on the empty corridor.

Quickly and quietly I reached the room door. I listened. A harsh, man's voice was swearing. An angry voice. The woman's voice explained and protested. I heard fear in the woman's voice. The vicious slap of a hard hand against flesh. Again. And again.

". . . kill both of you!"

I didn't hear the boy. Not a sound. Only the man's violent voice and the high sobs of the woman.

". . . teach you to run out on me!"

I put one hand on the small Colt under my suit coat and tried the door gently. It was locked. If I was going in, I was going to have to go the hard way.

But I wasn't going in.

"Take the hand out. Slow."

The voice was close behind me in the dim corridor of the shabby hotel. The gun was hard in my back. A gun barrel, or something round and hard like a gun barrel. I didn't turn around to find out. I took my hand out of my jacket.

"Walk."

I walked. To the stairs door, through and down, with the gun still in my back and the gunman's footsteps like an echo of mine on the worn marble of the old stairs. We came out through the second-floor door at the top of the iron-railed stairs and went down into the narrow lobby. The clerk smiled at me.

"Found the kid okay?"

I smiled. "I did, thanks."

"It's okay. Look, anythin' else I can do, just say the word. Okay?"

The happy clerk had liked the easy ten dollars, was hoping for more.

"Right," I smiled as I walked toward the doors.

Out in the deserted night of Clinton Street the gunman spoke softly behind me, "You got brains, man. That's good."

A car waited at the curb halfway along the dark block. It was the red Oldsmobile Cutlass I had seen twice in front of the Jurgens house in Douglaston. Someone was in the back seat. I couldn't make out the shadow clearly, but I had the feeling it could be a woman. The gunman prodded me to the front door. I opened it, got in. The gunman did not get in. The silent driver started the car, and we drove away.

North and then west through the night city, more people on the streets with each block toward the center of the island. The driver was a thick swarthy man with a black, drooping mustache who whistled off-key as he drove. Almost a soundless whistling. Some Latin rhythm. Was the woman in the back seat a Latin? If it was a woman. Maybe Puerto Rican?

There were fewer people on the streets again as we went farther west. By the time we reached the Hudson River and the dark streets in the shadow of the West Side Highway, the night was as silent and deserted as it had been on Clinton Street, and the Olds stopped. I felt the darkness and the emptiness and the silence somewhere inside me where I was scared. The driver sat with his hands on the wheel, still whistling his Latin melody silently and off-key.

A voice from the back seat said something in Spanish. It was a woman. A soft dark voice. Mezzo-soprano.

The driver got out of the car. He had a gun. He motioned me out. I got out and we walked through the blackness under the elevated highway toward the river.

Then I didn't hear the driver behind me. I turned to look. The driver was getting back into the car.

"Vaya con Dios," I said.

He looked at me. "Hey, you funny man, *hombre*."

The driver stared at me and I thought for a moment I might have been funny once too often. The woman in the back seat of the red Olds spoke. The driver shrugged. The car drove away.

It took me half an hour to walk out of the empty streets near the river to where I could hope to flag down a cab, and another twenty minutes to find an empty one that would take me back to the Lower East Side. It wasn't an area most cabbies want to go to at such a late hour.

He dropped me in the comparative safety of Second Avenue, and I had to walk the rest of the way to the Grace Hotel. The clerk almost jumped for joy when he saw me. He had visions of endless tens, and by now his dreams had made us old friends in his nighttime world. I asked him if Mrs. Garou and the boy were still in their room, and if he'd seen the guy who'd been with me earlier.

"Still in, far as I know," he said, half watching my face and half watching my hands to see if I was going to reach again for my wallet. "After you left, your friend went back up, too."

"He's still up there?"

"Sure is. I been watchin'. Sort of figured you'd want to know about anythin' they did."

His eagerness—his insignificant vision of sudden wealth—was pathetic, but it never hurts to have someone on your side, especially in a skidrow hotel. You never know when it might be useful. I dug out another ten.

"Keep your eyes open," I said, laid the ten on the desk. "What's your name?"

"Sam," he said, took the ten, grinned. "Sam Shurk."

I nodded seriously, we were partners. He was still grinning as I climbed the old marble-and-iron stairs to the second-floor door and went up to the third floor with its long, dim corridor. At this hour the seedy corridor with its peeling paint and bare wood was like something ten miles underground on a dead planet. Except for the sound of small feet running somewhere behind the walls. I moved as silently as the small animals, stood outside room 27.

This time there was no swearing inside. No sounds of violence. There was no sound at all. As silent behind the door as in the empty corridor. A partly open door. I looked at that door for some time. Just a few inches, but open. I got out my small gun and pushed the door open all the way.

It was a larger room than I had expected. Perhaps once, long ago when the Bowery had been "uptown," and America was still dreaming of its destiny, the Grace had been a real hotel, a comfortable haven for important visitors. A screen had been set up in the center to divide the room into sections, a single narrow iron bed in each section. The screen lay on its side now, and the room was empty.

Some of the drawers in the two battered bureaus were open. I opened the other drawers. They were all empty. A few hairpins, a dog-eared magazine, a boy's miniature racing car and, under a yellowed newspaper lining of a top drawer, one of those throwaway flyers they slip in suburban front doors to announce local events and/or sales. This one announced a fund-raising picnic and bike-a-thon for the Melville Aid Fund sponsored by the South Brooklyn Association next Sunday in Prospect Park. I didn't know what it was doing in a drawer a long way from South Brooklyn, and that was a good reason to put it into my pocket. When you have no explanation for something, it could be important.

There were two shallow closets. Both of them were empty. Except for a small stack of papers tied with a string and shoved far to the back of a closet top shelf. I fished them down, untied the string. They were publicity stills, a little yellow at the edges and with some of the gloss cracked, but still in good shape. Of an exotic go-go dancer up on a bar in a spangled G-string and with two sequined dots pasted over the nipples of her high breasts. She was a younger version of the woman I had seen with the boy in the lobby: Mrs. Garou. Younger, but the body not a lot different even now and in street clothes. I took a few of the prints.

A closed door opened into a bathroom shared by at least the next room. It stank, had a single window painted black, a broken sink and a chipped tub on claw legs, and it wasn't empty.

The dead man lay between the tub and the toilet, twisted in a heap as if thrown there. A young man wearing jeans, a decorated blue shirt and a black Windbreaker. Muscular but not big. Short, with good shoulders. A dark man with an Indian nose and black Indian eyes that stared up now at nothing. Latin. I had not seen the gunman who had walked me away from the room door and out of the hotel, but I had little doubt that I was seeing him now. He had come back up to the room, and for some reason that had killed him.

There was almost no blood on the bathroom floor. A trail of dark drops and smears led back out into the empty room. It stopped near one of the narrow iron beds. The heavy stain of blood had sunk into the age-darkened carpet, blended into the faded color and worn pattern. On the bed the pillow showed two powder-burned bullet holes. This killer had killed before. A killer who used a pillow to muffle the sound of his shots, hid the body in the bathroom, to prevent casual discovery and gain as much getaway time as possible.

I returned to the bathroom, put on the thin leather glove I always carry and lightly searched the body. He had been shot twice in the chest. There was no rigor mortis, he couldn't have been dead more than an hour or two. There were some bullets in his Windbreaker, but no gun anywhere. In his wallet a driver's license in the name of Luis Marquez, but no money or credit cards. Some change in his trouser pocket, a pack of small thin cigars and a matchbook from El Jazz Latino.

The second tie-in. I was on the right track of something. I didn't know what, and from now on I wouldn't be on this track alone. The clerk downstairs knew me now, I had to report the murder to the police, along with most of what I knew and had found. This time I had to tell them about the boy and hope that Lieutenant Guevara out in Douglaston wouldn't come down on me too hard.

The detectives came from Manhattan East like a commando force in enemy territory. It was skid row. Detective First Grade Lew Karnes was in charge. I knew him and he knew me. We don't like each other.

"From the top, Shaw."

I told him everything except that I had held out on Guevara about the boy, and I didn't give him any of my conclusions. He could make his own guesses. I gave him everything I'd found except the throwaway flyer from South Brooklyn. It had no obvious connection to the case anyway. He wrote it all down, looked at the body as the M.E. worked over it in the bathroom.

"What the hell was he doing this far downtown?"

Karnes was that kind of cop. Bigoted and obsolete. It had been a lot of years since all Latins huddled scared and under control above Ninety-sixth Street.

"So you traced the Garou kid here, but you don't know where he is now or what his connection is to the stiff out in Queens. There was a guy in this room slapped the Garou broad around, but you never saw him, don't know who he is or anything about him. Some spicks took you for a ride, but you don't know who they are. You're some detective."

You don't defend yourself against morons or argue with a cop like Karnes. So why did I do both?

"I haven't been on the case much longer than you, Karnes," I said. "I don't know who the dead man and his friends are yet, but I know they were watching the Jurgens house, and the dead man has to be the one who wanted me away from this room."

"You can't even prove that, you never saw the guy who moved you off. Sit over there and keep quiet."

I sat. Karnes followed his whole crew around, checking on them as they checked out the room and the corridor. Two patrolmen brought in my desk clerk. Karnes looked him over, saw that he was a small nobody, so leaned on him. He was that kind of cop, too.

"What's your name?"

"Shurk. Sam Shurk."

"Where'd the people in this room go, Shurk?"

"I don't know."

"You're the desk clerk. They checked out, didn't they?"

"No, sir, they never checked out."

"How much did the guy slip you to say that?"

"He didn't slip me nothin'!"

"But you saw him, didn't you?"

"No! I never saw no man. Just the woman and the kid."

"Tell me about *him*." Karnes pointed at me.

Shurk repeated what I had told Karnes about my actions at the hotel. Karnes jerked his head toward the bathroom. They were ready to zip the body into a body bag.

"That the guy who came down with Shaw?"

Sam Shurk looked into the bathroom. He looked away.

"That's him, yes."

"Who was he?"

"I don't know. I never seen him before. I thought he was a friend of Mr. Shaw."

Karnes raised an eyebrow. *"Mister* Shaw?"

"Him," Shurk said, nodded to me. He didn't have a sense of humor. I suppose not much had happened to him to help him develop one. Karnes was annoyed. People were supposed to laugh when he made a joke.

"Shit," Karnes said. "Now who was the man with the Garous?"

"I never saw no man with them."

"You don't know anything. How do all these people get into the hotel without passing the desk?"

"We got a back door, but it's locked."

"Let's see," Karnes said.

Shurk led us down to the lobby and past his registration desk, then through a door and along a darkened corridor to a heavy door at the far end. There were dingy cross corridors and dark rooms, mazelike, behind the lobby. The back door was unlocked. We all looked out into the dark alley. There was no one there. Not even a drunk.

"So we know how they all got in and out," Karnes said.

"I don't understand how it got open," Shurk said.

"Someone opened it," Karnes said. "You live in the hotel?"

"Yes," Sam Shurk said. "Back here."

"Then stay around."

He motioned to me. I followed him back out into the lobby. The M.E.'s men were carrying the body bag down the long flight of stairs from the second floor. Karnes morosely watched it go out.

"No way we'll ever trace that spick," he said. "They come, they go. Phony names and no address. Those Garous probably used a phony name, too, but we'll circulate the pic of the broad." He looked at the publicity shot of the woman as a go-go dancer, drooled more than a little. "Not bad, only I know every bar girl in the area, and I never saw her before. That saloon in the snap don't look local, neither. Probably the whole damned bunch are out-of-towners."

"They're in town now," I said. "They have to be somewhere."

"Sure, but not much chance finding 'em with what we got."

"You mind if I try?"

"Smart bastard! Get the hell out of here."

Stiff-necked and narrow-minded, he went back up the stairs to the second-floor door. I'd made a mistake and he wouldn't forget it. Sometimes you just can't give a damn. Before I left, I stopped at the desk to give Sam Shurk my card.

"If you see or hear anything I should know, call me. Anytime. My home number's on the card, too."

"Sure thing, Mr. Shaw." The eager assistant.

I walked the six blocks to where I had parked my Ferrari in a safe garage and drove uptown to my silent penthouse and welcome bed. Karnes had made me mad, but I knew he was right. Both murders were the kind that in a big city are too often never solved.

Six

I WOKE UP to October sunlight and the cook standing over the bed with a glass of orange juice. Maureen was on the phone. The cook glared at me over the orange juice, sure as always that a lout in my cheap profession would need something healthy in his stomach before he was in any condition to talk to his wife.

"I'll drink it in the kitchen," I said. "Now get out of here."

Maureen often wonders why the cooks tend to quit when she's away, they seem so content to her. They are. They always like her and hate me. I suspect all our cooks of being snobs, the genteel movie star dazzles them. I picked up the receiver to talk to my movie star. She still dazzles me, too.

"You're up early," I said.

"Our dear director's idea. To beat the heat out here. How are you, sweetheart?"

"Lonesome. When do you come home?"

"When do you come to Arizona?"

"Thayer's still out, I've got a new case."

"Oh, shit! Why do we go on like this, Paul? You don't have to work. Come out and be with me, please."

"And do what, Maurie? Read movie magazines all my life?"

"You were an actor, you can do a lot of things around a studio."

"I was an actor, not a P.R. man or a hairdresser."

"We'd be together, I wouldn't worry all day that some mad killer has shot you."

"No studio needs me except as Maureen Shaw's husband. My mad killers need me more."

She was silent at the other end of the line. I could hear many voices and a sense of echoing space. Dawn in Arizona with a movie company swinging into Hollywood gear.

"Paul? We'll go a month over schedule."

"Then I'll try to come out as soon as I wrap this one up."

"Paul Shaw, you're inhuman!"

"No, I'm not. Believe me."

"I'm glad," she said. I could hear her breathing, her lips close to the phone. "Suffer a lot, damn you."

"Work hard," I said. "Call you in a few days."

I lay in the bed for a time, my eyes closed, just listening to the sounds of the city far below our penthouse and thinking about Maureen. She is a redhead—rich dark red hair, thick and long. Spanish eyes, her voice low and throaty. A Hollywood voice, they love it. A small woman, slim; I can hold her in one hand, lift her. . . . I opened my eyes. Was I crazy? Because I had to at least pretend my work was important? No, not important, just mine. My work. I wasn't good enough to be an actor, Vietnam had taught me only one skill, so—a detective.

I got up. A detective is supposed to detect. I dressed. It was time to go back to the start out in Douglaston. I went into the kitchen, got my orange juice from the refrigerator while the cook ignored me. I sat down at the table.

"I'll have coffee now, one egg over light, two pieces of rye toast."

She snorted but went to work. I drank my first cup of coffee while she fried the egg. She made good coffee.

"You gonna be in for lunch or dinner?"

"Probably not," I said. "Dinner maybe."

She snorted again. Our cooks worked eight to eight, I won't have anyone in the apartment overnight, and sometimes I think they quit when Maureen's away not because they hate me, but because I'm rarely home and they go nuts alone. In a way I hoped this one wouldn't quit. She cooked a nice egg.

It was an Indian summer morning all across Queens, the orange and blue emptiness of Shea Stadium catching the crisp sunlight, the long inlets of the Sound shining as I reached the North Shore. The quiet street wasn't as quiet as it had been before an "event" had happened on it, neighbors and a lot of strangers gathered in gawking groups up and down the street. They all looked at my red Ferrari as it drove up to the Jurgens house. I looked for the red Olds. It wasn't there. The police car was, still parked in the driveway beside the house.

Sarah Jurgens opened her door. She seemed glad to see me, yet too distraught to say so or even care. Without speaking, she walked back into the living room as I closed the door. She sat down, hunched and shaky, her eyes afraid.

"I just can't believe it today," she said. "It's worse. Impossible. He can't be dead. Not in the daylight."

"I know," I said. "Has anything more happened?"

She shook her head. "They apologized because I can't

bury him yet. The police. I can't have the funeral yet, they're sorry."

"Does the name Garou mean anything to you? Ted Garou, maybe some other first name? Maybe a woman's name?"

"No," she said. "I hate funerals. I don't want to have a funeral. I don't care if they keep . . . the body."

"A go-go dancer and her son?"

She shook her head again. "I have to bury him, though, don't I? I have to have a funeral."

"Luis Marquez? A bunch of Latins in a red Oldsmobile?"

"I don't know." She shook her head violently. "Who are they? All those names? I don't know any of those people."

Her blond hair swung in the sunlight as she shook her head repeatedly the way a child does, overemphatically carried away by the physical action. I told her about the people in the red Olds watching the house, how I'd found Ted Garou, the murder of Luis Marquez and the other events of yesterday and last night. The weight of it seemed to press her down. Her head no longer moved, the blond hair half hiding her face.

"What's happening, Paul? What does it all mean?"

"None of it means anything to you?"

"Nothing."

"They all seem to be connected to your husband somehow," I said. "It looks like they meant something to him."

She stood, walked around the sunny living room.

"Then there's something I didn't know about my husband. A lot I didn't know. Perhaps I didn't really know him at all."

She was wearing a green shirtwaist dress now. A simple

dress that swung with the movement of her youthful body. The room seemed so much larger in the daylight than it had the night Matt Jurgens had died. I thought about that night as I watched the dress swing lightly against her slim body.

She stopped walking. "I can't go through a funeral. I just can't." She smiled. An almost girlish smile. "Will you help me, Paul?"

"Not with a funeral," I said.

Maybe she, too, was thinking about the night before when we had been alone in this room. After they had taken the body of Matt Jurgens away. She came to lean against me, her blond head down.

"I need help," she said. "For more than the funeral."

She held my shoulders tight, her face against my chest.

"You hired me to find who killed your husband. I'll do my job."

"I suppose you will."

She looked up at me, put her arms around my neck.

"Don't you want me to find the killer?"

She pressed against me, her body as firm and tight under the thin dress as it was slim and youthful. She took very good care of her body, and that took time. A lot of time and work.

"I don't know what I want," she said. "I don't know how I feel anymore. I wish none of it had ever happened, and I wish I could forget that it happened. Forget everything except myself."

"You wish Matt was still with you?"

She studied my face. "I'm not sure."

"You keep yourself in very good shape."

"I'm glad you like it."

"It takes time, work."

"When you're alone as much as I've been, you have

plenty of time. You keep busy. You hope that someday someone might come along who appreciates all your effort.''

She moved her body against me. Softly. I was ready to take her upstairs, pick her up and carry her up to any bed I could find. Forget that I had a job to do, that somewhere outside the sunny, silent house there was a killer.

The ring of the doorbell shattered the silence. I stepped away. Sarah Jurgens didn't. She stood there in the living room as if still clinging to me.

Estelle Jellicoe swept into the room.

''Nobody answered the door, so I just let myself in, Sarah, dear. Oh, you poor girl, what a terrible tragedy! I'd have been over yesterday, but Peter was so busy in the office I just could *not* get away. Are you all right? What can I do? It must be awful for you. Alone in this house. When Mr. Shaw isn't here, I mean. Why not come and stay with me for a few weeks?''

The quick comment on my being there showed that she hadn't missed Sarah clinging to me as she had come in. And her concern was all hollow. All hollow and she made it obvious. She didn't give a damn about Sarah, and she didn't care if Sarah knew it. She even wanted Sarah to know it. The two women did not love each other, and sympathy wasn't what had brought Estelle Jellicoe here. Neither sympathy nor shared sorrow for the death of her brother. I was pretty sure she hadn't cared any more for her brother than she did for his wife.

''I'm all right here, Estelle,'' Sarah Jurgens said. The soft slow warmth was gone from her voice.

''I do hope so, dear,'' Estelle smiled. ''But you will have a lot to do the next few weeks. With the house, the funeral, all your personal affairs to settle. Why not let Peter handle the office? Give him your proxies and power of attorney, and you won't have to even think about the office. Peter will be taking charge anyway with poor Matt gone.''

''Peter's not even a department head,'' Sarah said.

''We want to keep full control in the family, dear, and you or I can't run an advertising agency.''

''Why not?'' Sarah said.

Estelle smiled. ''You really don't have the abilities, Sarah, and I have a financial stake in the success of the business.''

Sarah's voice took on an edge, cool and hard. ''I didn't live with Matt without learning about the agency, and Harry Glanz will tell me what I don't know, handle the day-to-day details. It's what Matt suggested if anything happened to him.''

''How nice, you even inherit Matt's job. But Harry Glanz is an old woman, and you still know nothing about advertising.''

''I can run a business a lot better than Junior Jellicoe! Matt never did think Junior was worth a hill of beans.''

''Matt was stupid! The way he was going he'd have run the agency into the ground. It's been stagnating for years.''

The two women glared at each other across the living room, where shadows had begun to cross the bright October sunlight as clouds built up somewhere outside to the east.

''We'll see what the officers and directors have to say,'' Estelle Jellicoe said.

''Don't forget the lawyers,'' Sarah said. ''I own an outright majority now, thanks to brother Bill. It's my company, Estelle.''

''Perhaps legally, but you'll find out soon enough that you can't run it, the people won't work for you.''

''We'll see, won't we?''

Estelle Jellicoe stood in the darkening room as if about to say something else, but it never came. The hate, clear between them, wasn't new. An old war, matured over many years, and Estelle Jellicoe turned without even a nod to her sister-in-law and walked out of the room. The outside door slammed.

"You two don't love each other," I said.

"Estelle doesn't love anyone except herself and maybe Junior Jellicoe," Sarah said. "Matt could never stand her."

"You didn't tell me Peter worked at Matt's agency."

"I suppose I didn't think about it," she said. "I was confused that night, and Peter isn't important anyway. Matt only hired him for Estelle's sake. Junior isn't that bright, and Matt said he had no talent for P.R. or advertising."

"He doesn't seem to know that."

"I think he does inside. It's Estelle who doesn't know it, I suppose because he's her only chance of running the agency."

"How important would it be to her that Peter become top man at the agency?"

"Very," Sarah said, "but he won't be top man."

"He's trying hard," I said and described what I'd seen and heard at the agency yesterday. "The whole place feels like a South American country about to have a coup d'état."

"I'll stop that, and fast!" She almost snarled it out, and I saw the claws of another side of her, a side that wanted more than a husband to pay attention to her. A side of her Estelle Jellicoe didn't seem to have been aware of, a new factor in any power struggle at the agency. "It's *my* agency now!"

"The whole show?" I said.

She heard the question in my voice and suddenly smiled at me. Shoulders down, she shook her head.

"Listen to me. Being tough. It's going to take more than legal ownership to run the agency, isn't it?"

"It usually does."

She came to me again, put her arms up around my neck. "Help me, Paul. You know people, you can judge work. We could be a hell of a team."

"My wife probably wouldn't like it," I said, which was only partly true. Maureen wouldn't like all Sarah Jurgens seemed to have in mind, but she'd love me to try the agency business or any business that wasn't the detective business.

"All right," Sarah said, "you're married." She dropped her arms from my neck, found a cigarette in a box on the coffee table. She lighted the cigarette. "That could be fixed."

"You don't know my wife."

She laughed. "I'll work on it."

"Which is what I'm supposed to be doing," I said. "I'll be in touch."

Seven

I DROVE BACK into the city with heavy clouds chasing me all the way. The sky was building to real October, the temperature diving, and the day growing grayer. By the time I reached the office of Jurgens Associates, a cold rain had begun to fall. The temperature was cooler inside the agency, too.

The new receptionist gave me the frosty eyes. An older woman than the departed Carmen and definitely Anglo. She had neat reddish hair, neat Peck & Peck clothes and a neat upper-middle-class accent. A college woman down on her luck, one way or another, and she tried to smile, but it was hard.

"May I help you?"

"If you can tell me where to find Peter Jellicoe."

"*Mister* Jellicoe is busy." She wasn't even trying to smile now. "Perhaps someone else?"

"Busy taking over?" I said. "Did Jellicoe hire you?"

Her smile wasn't even a memory. "If you'll tell me your business, *sir,* I'm sure someone will handle it for you."

"Just tell *Mister* Jellicoe that Paul Shaw is here for Sarah Jurgens. He'll figure it all out."

"Jurgens?"

"Forgot to tell you about Mrs. Jurgens, did he? She owns the agency, right? I'm working for her. Ring Jellicoe."

Flustered and more than a little confused, she called Jellicoe, talked for a moment or two, then told me to go up to the president's office. She was annoyed and red faced. Peter Jellicoe had just lost a lot of standing in her eyes.

I went up to the big, almost empty, office where Matt Jurgens had worked. No longer bare and Spartan, it had files and papers strewn all over the couch and chairs, and Peter Jellicoe large behind the old desk. Sullen behind the dead man's desk as if aware that I had just lost him face with his new receptionist.

"Tell my Aunt Sarah we've got an agency to run," he said angrily. "Tell her to call before she sends anyone here."

"You tell her," I said. "I've got a pair of murders to solve. What do you know about a boy named Ted Garou?"

"Never heard of him."

"Small, skinny, pale, lives with his mother."

Jellicoe shook his head. I showed him the go-go photo I'd found in the room at the Grace Hotel. He said he didn't know the woman, and unlike Detective Karnes didn't seem interested. Too young or too much the straight arrow.

"New Orleans," I said. "Nineteen sixty-six and Ted Garou. It all meant something to Matt Jurgens."

"I wasn't even at the agency in sixty-six," Peter Jellicoe said. He was motionless behind the desk. Not swiveling, or tilting, or doodling, or turning a pencil, or rubbing his nose, or even swinging a leg. He seemed to have no nervous habits at all. Controlled? Or stolid, unimaginative? I didn't know which. "Hell, I was only fourteen in sixty-six. But Matt took trips all over even then. He was probably in New Orleans lots of times."

"But you've never seen that boy? You're sure?"

"I'm sure." His voice was quick and certain, but then he sat forward behind the desk as if he'd just heard something. He had. I realized that his mind was no more involved in the business of the agency than Matt Jurgens's mind had been. Even now his attention was somewhere else, and he had just registered what I had said some minutes ago. "A pair of murders? You said you had a pair of murders to solve?"

I told him about last night and the shooting of Luis Marquez at the Grace Hotel on skid row. "Does the name Luis Marquez mean anything to you?"

"Not a thing," he said, still leaning toward me behind the desk, his voice puzzled and something else—interested. "What's Uncle Matt's connection to all of that? Skid row? Someone named Marquez? A Puerto Rican nightclub and a pawned bracelet? It doesn't make much sense, Shaw."

Before I could chase that one around, the office door swept open and Estelle Jellicoe flowed in. She was a woman who did nothing by halves. Neither entering a room nor getting angry. I could tell by her eyes and grim mouth that she was still in a fury over her confrontation with Sarah Jurgens, had come to rage about it to her son. But when she saw me, the mask of a smiling public facade dropped over her angular face.

"Mr. Shaw," she said, sweeping papers from an armchair, sitting down, swinging a rapid leg. "You appear everywhere. Is that being a good detective?"

Peter told her everything I had told him about last night and skid row. She was as interested as he had been and more eager than puzzled by it all. She thought hard in the armchair, her leg no longer swinging, and something seemed to mean a lot to her.

"What could any of that have to do with Matt?" She studied my face. "What was he up to?"

It was the same thing that had seemed to be on Peter Jellicoe's mind. They were a close team. Probably because her husband had gone. It couldn't be too good for Peter's marriage.

"That's my job, to find out," I said. "You two seem pretty close. Unusual these days. Mother and son."

"Listen—" Peter began, leaning toward me again.

"Only in business, Mr. Shaw," Estelle said icily. "It's my company and my son. We have our interests to consider."

"It was Matt's company," I said. "Now it's Sarah's."

"We'll see about that!" Estelle said. "Damn it, Matt was nowhere near carrying his weight in the agency anymore! Peter says he neglected the whole agency the last few years. Soon he'd have run it right into the ground! Hiring creatures like that Carmen, going off on his trips and coming back with no damned business at all, even losing some of his own accounts. Peter and the others have been carrying Matt for years, and a change is long overdue."

"And Peter is the change?" I said.

"Yes! We're sorry that Matt is dead, but Peter is family and can do the job!"

I looked toward Peter Jellicoe. He was looking down at the desk, moodily poking at something with a pencil. "It's a family company. There's only me.'

His voice didn't sound thrilled. I wondered how long his mother had been telling him that "when Uncle Matt's gone, there's only you." Estelle Jellicoe seemed to read my mind. She didn't like what she read.

"And Peter won't run the company like a private king-dom," she said. "He says Matt even took fifty thousand dollars out of the office recently. In cash. No one knows what for."

"He could do that?"

Peter nodded. "Boss and president and owner. It looks as if he just plain took it home."

"And you knew that?"

"I knew," Peter said.

I watched both of them. "Was the money found? Did you ask Sarah?"

"We're not sure," Estelle said. "Sarah didn't mention any money to me."

She sounded almost pleased. Peter Jellicoe shook his head when I looked at him. They didn't know what had happened to the fifty thousand dollars. So they were say-ing.

The short, rumpled pipe smoker who stopped me in the corridor outside the president's office said that he didn't know where the fifty thousand dollars was, either. He had been waiting for me in the corridor. Hand out, nodding toward another door.

"Harry Glanz. Sarah told me she hired you and to give you all the help I could. Come on into my office."

Across the hall, his office was smaller and more com-fortable. Lived in, even if for only eight hours or so a day. He waved me to a high-backed wing chair. I asked him at once about the fifty thousand dollars and what Matt had wanted it for. He didn't know what Matt Jurgens had wanted fifty thousand dollars for.

"But you knew Matt had taken it from the office?"

"Everyone knew. Our bookkeeper likes Peter."

"You're a vice-president, number-two man, and Matt didn't tell you why he needed so much cash?"

"Number-two man only technically," Glanz smiled. He relighted his pipe. "I'm an inside man: writing, editing, layout, some idea work. Inside men don't run agencies. Salesmen, account execs, the ones who bring in the business, they run agencies. The outside men. Inside men like me are just overhead."

"But you're in command now?"

He smiled again. "Only nominally. Peter is family, and Estelle is lining up everyone behind him."

"Can she?"

"If Sarah goes along, it's certain."

"And if Sarah doesn't go along with Peter?"

He puffed on his pipe. It was one of those with a briar bowl on top of a duralumin body. It cleaned the tars out of the smoke and kept the spit from the smoker's mouth. Glanz puffed for some time, then spoke through the smoke.

"They might convince the board, even the staff, that Peter can run the show better than anyone else. That Sarah never has shown any interest in the business, not even socially."

"The 'Duchess of Douglaston'?"

He laughed aloud this time. "She has been cool and aloof. No one here really knows her except me. Not that I blame her, with Matt always away on the road. He never made much effort to bring her into the agency circle."

"But she owns the company now. What she wants she'll get, won't she?"

Glanz puffed harder on the odd pipe. A Kirsten, made out in Washington state. I could hear the tar and saliva gurgle inside it. He took it out of his mouth.

"If the board opposed her, and the staff refused to work for her, she wouldn't own very much. If the staff all quit, the accounts would probably go with them, and there wouldn't be any agency to own. Not really. It'd be hard to get replacements if the whole staff walked out.''

That put a different angle on Peter and Estelle Jellicoe. Maybe they knew what they were doing.

''Peter Jellicoe says Matt wasn't bringing in much business from his trips lately.''

Glanz puffed again. ''Not too much.''

''Could he have been doing something on the road besides agency business?''

Glanz shrugged. ''If he was, it wasn't anything new. He never sold as well on the road as he should have. Of course, Matt selling at half what he should did better than most selling at all they could, so no one said much about it.''

''That's all? Just seemed to sell less than expected?''

''Some pretty careless lapses here and there. You know, clients not seen, appointments not kept, sometimes hard to get in touch with him in whatever city he was in.''

''All along? I mean, since he started the agency?''

''I'd say so. He was always offhand, easygoing. Only maybe more so lately.''

I asked him about Ted Garou and Luis Marquez. He said he didn't know them. I described them, asked about the Grace Hotel, skid row, El Jazz Latino and the pawnshop. He shook his head to all of it, looked more and more unhappy as I went on. His pipe had gone out, and he chewed on it.

''What the hell was Matt doing? Mixed up in places like those? I'm not sure I believe it. Some mistake. Maybe you're way off on the wrong track, Shaw.''

''Maybe,'' I agreed, ''but right now I don't have any other track to be on. Can you give me any ideas about who would want Matt Jurgens dead? Or why?''

He tapped out his dead pipe. "Beyond Peter and Estelle maybe, or Sarah herself, I can't think of anyone who gains."

"No new client he was having big trouble with?"

"No new clients at all."

"What about the Jellicoes? They're working overtime to take control now, but how about before? Could they have murdered Matt to get the agency?"

For a question like that Glanz needed his pipe. He filled it from a leather pouch, a deep brown-and-black tobacco with a delicious odor. The pure taste and comfort of a pipe is one of the saddest victims of cancer. Glanz had other problems.

"Peter was on very thin ice with Matt all this year," he said slowly now. "They never got along too well because of Estelle pushing the boy all the time, and because Matt never thought Peter was much good at the work. When Bill Jurgens died, I got the vice-presidency, and Estelle was furious. A year ago Matt hired a new media manager from outside instead of promoting Peter. That really enraged Estelle, and Peter and Matt were arguing all year. There was whispering that Matt had had it, that Peter was going to be fired. I wouldn't have been surprised, only Matt never mentioned the possibility to me."

"Would he have mentioned it to you?"

"Well, not necessarily."

"So they could have had a real motive?"

"I suppose so." His voice seemed reluctant, as if he really didn't want to say it. But he said it.

I said, "How about you?"

"Me?" His pipe seemed to hang in the air at the end of his arm as he stared at me.

"Sarah said that maybe she could run the agency with

your help. That would make you the big man around here. With any luck you might be able to pressure her into giving you a piece of the action.''

After a time he nodded, put the shiny pipe back into his mouth. ''It's a really dirty business you're in, isn't it?''

——— **Eight** ———

IN THE AGENCY RECEPTION ROOM I used the telephone to call Lew Karnes at Manhattan East and ask what he'd found so far. The new receptionist watched me. She wasn't yet sure who was who in the business, who she should work at getting close to, and she didn't like that. Lew Karnes told me to get lost and hung up. When I called back, they told me Karnes had left the squad room.

Out in my car I thought about calling Sid Bender, our lawyer, to put pressure on some assistant D.A. to get Manhattan East to let us do our job. But I decided to hold off in the hope that Karnes would cool down and took out the flyer I'd found in the room at the Grace Hotel where Ted Garou and his mother had lived and Luis Marquez had died. "The South Brooklyn Association Announces a Fund-Raising Picnic and Bike-A-Thon for The Melville Aid Fund." The address of the South Brooklyn Association was on Emmons Avenue in Sheepshead Bay.

I took the Brooklyn-Battery tunnel and the Belt Parkway around Brooklyn past the Verrazano Bridge and Gravesend Bay to the Coney Island Avenue off ramp. The headquarters of the South Brooklyn Association was a simple storefront across from the party-boat piers and two blocks down from the closed Lundy's Restaurant. Old man Lundy, who had owned most of the real estate on the waterfront, had died recently, and everyone in the fishing village inside the city was nervously waiting to see what was going to happen next. At the South Brooklyn Association the only one waiting was a plump, eager gray-haired lady behind a desk in the long, barren store. She beamed at me.

"Can I help?"

"I'm looking for some information about the Melville Fund," I said. "The picnic and bike-a-thon?"

Her eager beaming plunged all the way down to barely held-back tears. "Oh, it's so sad. That poor little boy. We all decided it was the least we could do."

"Very sad," I said. "Just what is it? About the boy?"

"Leukemia," she whispered as if just saying the dread word aloud were infectious. "The worst kind, I'm afraid. He has so little time unless he can have a very delicate operation. We're hoping to raise the entire cost."

"A local boy?" I said.

"Oh, yes. This is entirely a neighborhood project. His poor mother and father have no money, you know. That's why they came to the city, so Mr. Melville could get work. He's in the construction trade, and building is so slow now."

"How much have you raised so far?"

"Only a few thousand dollars, I'm afraid." Dejected, she immediately revived and beamed again. "But we have great hopes for the picnic and bike-a-thon. They're such a nice little family and so cheerful around the neighborhood. Are you going to sponsor a rider in our bike-a-thon or just buy some picnic tickets?"

"I'll take a picnic ticket," I said.

"One?"

"One. And the Melvilles' address."

"Oh, we don't give out their address. Their privacy is so precious to them now." She blinked, smiled up at me. A gray-haired Kewpie doll, the picture of everyone's grandmother. "Of course, I'm sure they'd want to meet anyone who sponsored, say, five riders or bought a block of ten tickets."

The tickets were five dollars each. There's something of the blackmail artist in all of us, if not the con man. I didn't see the connection between the Melvilles, Ted Garou and his mother and Matt Jurgens, the Garous had probably just picked up the flyer somewhere, but I had to check it out. I parted with the fifty bucks reluctantly. The old lady didn't seem to mind.

They were typical row houses on a quiet side street six blocks up from the bay itself. Semidetached, with driveways on each side, garages behind, and even some canvas sun awnings still out until the real cold set in. Two families to a building, enclosed front porches, postage-stamp-size front and back yards. A blue-collar neighborhood, mostly Irish or Italian once and perhaps still, but that would be less certain now, and less completely ethnic.

I rang the front doorbell of the Melville house. It was in the center of the block, shades drawn and silent, with no sign of life on the glassed-in porch or anywhere else. There was an aura of neglect about it: brown grass, hard and empty flower beds, no curtains at the windows. I went on ringing. No one answered.

I tried the door. It was locked. I glanced around to be sure I was alone before trying a credit card on the lock or using a picklock. I wasn't alone. A hard-eyed old woman stood on the glassed-in porch of the other half of the semidetached and watched me. Across the driveway the curtains moved at a first-floor window of the next house. The neighbors seemed to be protecting the Melvilles. I smiled and nodded to the hard-eyed old woman on the other porch.

"The Melvilles!" I called. "Not home?"

She nodded but went on watching me. I walked back to my little Ferrari. I drove to the next corner, turned right and went on for a few blocks until I came to a dead end at the edge of the salt marshes of Jamaica Bay.

The rain that had stopped when I came out of Jurgens Associates had started again, thin and cold on a sea wind. I lighted a cigarette and watched the bleak windswept bulrushes and muddy channels that wound out to the open water. I thought of nothing in particular for a time, just smoked and watched the rain and the blowing rushes and the gulls wheeling in the gray sky. A great blue heron stepped slow and high through the muddy water. I thought of Maureen in Arizona. No rain or great blue herons in Arizona. I hoped she was thinking about me.

I finished the cigarette, flicked it out into the rain, then drove back the way I had come, circled the block behind the Melville house and parked up in the next block. I got my raincoat out of the trunk, a snap-brim fedora and a pair of glasses with plain window glass for lenses. It should be enough disguise for watchful neighbors. I walked slowly through the cold rain toward the Melville house again.

The blue car arrived before I got there.

An old powder-blue Datsun sedan with rusted bumpers and one dented fender that turned into the driveway of the Melvilles' half of the semidetached. The car looked as neglected as the house. The man who got out was short, burly and heavy shouldered, with a bull neck and the close-cropped hair of an old-fashioned Marine drill instructor. He wore stained, torn and faded work clothes, heavy work

boots. His walk as he went up the driveway toward the
rear of the house was light for such a ponderous man,
quick and gliding, like a deceptively fast tank crossing a
rice paddy. He vanished behind the house.

I stopped beside the telephone pole in front of the house,
and lighted another cigarette, slow and casual, cupping
my hands against the rain and watching the semidetached
over them. No lights went on in the Melville house despite
the gloomy day. I walked on, turned into the driveway of
another dark house four doors up and slipped back over
the low rear fences to the backyard of the Melville house.

The battered blue Datsun was still in the driveway at
the side, and there was still no light anywhere in the house.
I went up the back-porch stairs slowly and softly. Through
the rear windows the kitchen was empty, but now I saw a
pale blue glow from the living room beyond the arch into
the kitchen. Someone was watching television in the living
room.

There was no way I could get close to the living room,
so I went back down and looked through the Datsun. Its
interior was as battered as its exterior, the car of a man
who rode hard and cared little. Cigarette butts overflowed
the dash ashtray, littered the floor. Empty Coors beer cans
were heaped on the rear seat, and two unopened six-packs
stood on the floor. The glove compartment held a dog-
eared travel guide stamped with the address of a gas station in Louisiana and a big Smith & Wesson .357 Magnum
revolver. On the floor under the glove compartment I found
a matchbook from El Jazz Latino.

I closed the car door. Now I really wanted a closer look
at the man who had driven the Datsun. Down the driveway
toward the street the garbage cans were set up against the
side of the house directly under some side windows. I

climbed carefully on top of one can, thankful for my height. On tiptoe I could just see into the living room.

The thick man sprawled in an armchair, legs straight out, feet splayed in the heavy work shoes, staring at the television. There was no other light in the room, as if the man preferred the half-light of a gray day. He held a can of Coors in his broad hand, sucked at it from time to time without looking at it. A crushed beer can lay at his feet, a six-pack with four full ones stood next to the chair. The eyes that stared toward the TV were pale and empty. Light eyes and all surface as if the brain behind them had gone dark, switched off like an engine idling out of gear. The eyes of a man thinking of nothing at all.

It's not easy to think of nothing, however briefly. To have a totally blank mind neither in nor out of the world. I'd seen that look only twice before. On a hired killer waiting on death row for the gas chamber the next morning and on a sergeant in Vietnam who could kill ten Cong in an afternoon and not remember even raising his weapon. His brain shut off when he killed in hot action, on a different level of being.

Now, balanced on the garbage can in the gray afternoon rain, I watched the silent man sprawled in his worn work clothes in the dim blue light of the TV. His hand moved to raise the beer can, drain it, crush it between the fingers, drop it to the floor, reach down for another can. All without a flicker in the pale eyes, without the movement of a muscle in the expressionless face. There was something animal about him, inexorable. The eyes of a snake, the impassive face of some jungle cat. Even when the telephone rang, his thick hand seemed to reach out detached, not part of him, moving toward the receiver on its own. . . .

On the garbage can I ducked down and looked quickly

behind me. Call it E.S.P., a hunch, luck. A short skinny little man stood at the window of the next pair of semi-detached houses, his eyes on me, and the telephone in his hand. I could be wrong, but I didn't wait to find out. I ran across the backyard, over the low fence, through the next yard and out into the next street. I turned right and kept on running. I didn't look back. No fancy tricks, just full speed to my little Ferrari.

Then I looked back. No one was behind me or anywhere else in sight through the cold October rain. I was considering whether to stay and watch the house from the car or get out of there when I saw him. He came down the driveway at the side of the semidetached with that gliding walk that seemed slow but wasn't. Hatless, without a coat, he stood and looked up and down the street through the rain. He looked toward me and the Ferrari. I got out of there.

Nine

THE RAIN CHASED ME all the way back along Gravesend Bay and the Narrows. And not just the rain. There was something about the silent man that made me feel colder than the October rain. It made me drive faster than I liked to the Battery Tunnel and up the rain-slick F.D.R. Drive. I wanted to know who the man was, where he fitted with Matt Jurgens—if he did—and with the Garous and the Melvilles and with all the rest of what I didn't know enough about.

I took the exit at Houston, turned north on First Avenue, swung around the block on Seventh Street and Third Avenue and back along St. Marks. The blue Datsun of the silent beer drinker had had a .357 Magnum in it, a travel guide from Louisiana where New Orleans was and another matchbook from El Jazz Latino. I kept on coming back to the cellar club, one way or another, as if somehow it stood at the center of it all.

In the midafternoon no one was sweeping the wet concrete terrace, and the club would not open for some hours. But there was a distant light inside, and the door was unlocked. I went in.

Across the big tomblike room with its small tables

jammed between the concrete-covered steel-beam columns in front of the bandstand, four people sat at the long bar side by side with a fifth near the tables behind them. Even as I entered, the man behind the four at the bar hurried off into the shadows toward the rest rooms at the rear. I took his place behind the four at the bar. They didn't turn. Except for the drinks in front of them they could have been waiting for a bus.

"Matt Jurgens still dead, *amigo?*"

He was first on the left of the four, the gray-haired owner with the lean Castilian face on the short, broad body. The Cholo accent was only partly there now, just enough to let me know I was still an unwelcome Anglo.

"So is Luis Marquez," I said.

The middle-aged mop man who had admired our Madison Avenue address was next to the owner. He started to turn toward me. Number three on the bar stools, a small dark woman I didn't know, put her hand on the mop man's arm. He sat back again.

"Marquez?" the owner said. "It is always sad to hear of the death of a fellow Latino. How did this happen?"

His accent was all gone now. He'd made his point. I told him what had happened to Luis Marquez and where.

"Garou?" he said. "French?"

"Probably Cajun, from New Orleans," I said. "You know the boy, maybe? Or his mother? Did they come in here? She works go-go clubs. Maybe you saw the boy around Matt Jurgens?"

"No," the owner said. "We don't know the boy."

"Maybe around the Jurgens Associates office?" I said, nodding to the fourth person at the long bar, the former receptionist at the agency. Carmen of the Indian-looking eyes and wide smile. She wasn't smiling now, her face showed blank in the mirror.

"No," Carmen said. "We never heard of no Garou."

"Did you meet Matt Jurgens in here, Carmen?"

"No."

"But you did know him before you got the job."

"Around," she said. "He needed a good receptionist."

"And he came in here a lot. Why?"

The owner said, "Why was this Luis Marquez shot? By whom?"

He spoke better English than I did when he wanted to. I'd like to have known more about him, but if I asked, I'd probably just get the broken English.

"I don't know," I said. "He was after the Garous for some reason. Maybe he tailed me to them or was watching them on his own, I don't know yet. There was a man with them when I found them in that room last night. I didn't see him. Later, after I found Marquez, I also found an ad flyer in the room." I told them about Brooklyn, the Melville Aid Fund and the man I'd seen at the Melville semi-detached. "He had a gun in the car, a Louisiana travel guide and a matchbook from this club. He could be the man with the Garous at the hotel."

The small woman I didn't know, who sat between the mop man and Carmen in the row at the bar and had said nothing up to now, spoke into the bar mirror. Her face was half hidden by the shadow of her dark hair.

"You know the name of this man?"

"No," I said.

"You know what he does? What he is? Why he's in New York?"

"No."

"A blue Datsun," the nameless woman said. "You know the license number?"

"No." I'd left too fast to take it down.

The mop man said, "You some detective, *amigo*. You don' know nothin'."

"Describe this man again," the woman said.

I did. "Did any of you see him here in your club?"

The small woman with the long dark hair didn't answer. She was no longer looking into the mirror but was staring down at her drink, her face totally hidden by the shadow of her long hair. I still hadn't really seen her face, only the flash of one dark eye, a slim nose, pale coffee-colored skin.

"No," the owner said. "He wasn't in here."

"You feature jazz," I said. "He's from Louisiana, maybe New Orleans. He could be a musician."

"Not in this club," the mop man said.

"He wouldn't be easy to miss," I said.

"He was never in the club," the owner said.

"Okay," I said, "maybe he got the matches from Luis Marquez. I figure he got Luis's gun, maybe shot him with it. Luis was killed with a smaller gun than a Magnum. Tell me about Luis Marquez. Who was he? What was he doing in the Grace Hotel?"

"Luis Marquez?" the owner said. "Marquez? Who's he?"

"Just another poor Latino," the mop man said.

The small nameless woman said nothing.

"Another damn spick killing," Carmen said.

"You seen one P.R., you seen 'em all," the owner said.

For a moment, when I'd been talking about the man in front of the TV in Brooklyn, I'd had them with me. Now they were gone again, and once more I was just Señor Charlie, the Anglo. While I was trying to think of some way to prove I was their friend, noble and without prejudice, a movement in the shadows at the rear of the vast room caught my eye. Someone slipped quickly across the rear of the club up to a side door and out into what had to be an alleyway.

I got only a fast glimpse of the man, but it was enough. Peter Jellicoe. I sprinted to the side door and out. The alley was already empty.

The alley gave not onto St. Marks Place but onto Ninth Street. With luck I could take a little extra time and still catch Peter Jellicoe. I went back to the four of them lined up in front of the bar mirror like a row of bronze Buddhas with their backs to me.

"What did Peter Jellicoe want here?"

"Who?" the owner said.

"Ain't nobody in here, man," the mop man said. "We ain't open yet, *sí?*"

"Okay," I said, "I know the routine. How about you, Carmen? You can't tell me you don't know Jellicoe. What did he want in here?"

"Mr. Jellicoe? Was he in here? I must have got in too late to give him a kiss."

I had no more time if I was going to have a chance at picking up Jellicoe. I went out the front into the thinning rain and gray afternoon light of St. Marks Place. Most likely Jellicoe was parked somewhere along St. Marks and would have to circle around from Ninth Street through the afternoon crowd on the avenues. I leaned back inside a recessed doorway and watched up and down the wet street. With the rain easing it was already getting colder, and I shivered inside my light raincoat. Shivered, waited, hoped I was right. I was.

Peter Jellicoe came along the opposite side of the street from the direction of Second Avenue. Furtive. Moving slowly and watching across to the side of the street where El Jazz Latino was and where I stood hidden. The big adman looked like a lumbering bird ready to fly at the slightest alarm. He'd seen me in the club, was uncertain whether I'd seen him or not and hoped that if I had seen him, I'd gone off somewhere so that he could get back to his car. Nervous. Six-foot-four, two hundred and ten pounds, more than just handsome, trying to avoid being seen on an open street by simply walking on the opposite side. I wasn't sure if I should laugh or cry.

I did neither. They both made noise. I didn't move, only watched from the doorway until I saw him stop on the far side of the busy street, take a long look up and down the street, but with eyes so preoccupied with himself that he didn't really look at all and wouldn't have seen me if I'd been in front of him. Then he crossed the street through the crawling traffic to a powerful black Porsche convertible with its top up against the now stopped October rain. He was smiling. He was safe. I was nowhere around in the mob of faceless people. He had outfoxed me. Just like on any TV show.

In my Ferrari I didn't follow too closely. There was no need. On crosstown streets the traffic inched bumper to bumper, if I lost the Porsche at one light, I'd catch it at the next. On the avenues the cars, trucks, buses and bicycles moved faster but in a great phalanx between the staggered lights, and there was no way to lose the Porsche unless Jellicoe spotted me, which he never would. He didn't and the trip was short. To the Grace Hotel.

I half-circled the block to a narrow alley that cut back through to just across the street from the Grace Hotel. The Porsche was in the shabby parking lot of the hotel—a narrow space where a building had been torn down, surrounded by one wall of the hotel and two other buildings, and blacktopped. In any big city, walls are irresistible to anyone with chalk, crayon, paintbrush or spray can, and all three walls and the blacktop were covered with violent scrawls, grotesque and obscene. In any big city, an empty space is automatically a refuse dump, and the narrow lot was littered with the dregs of things drunk, eaten, smelled, smoked, worn and abandoned.

As I watched, Peter Jellicoe got out of his Porsche. He stood for a moment beside it, looking at the scrawled and littered little parking lot like a man who was appalled by what he saw, or nervous at being where he was, or uneasy that he might be seen here, or all three. Whichever it was, he shook himself and hurried out of the lot, turned left and into the front door of the Grace Hotel. I locked my Ferrari, crossed to the alley on the far side of the Grace and slipped around to the rear door. It was unlocked. Again or still, I didn't know which. I examined the lock. It was broken internally. I went inside.

The maze of narrow corridors and dark rooms behind the registration desk was dim and silent. A single bare bulb burned in the main corridor, a feeble twenty-five watt or less at the far end of each cross corridor. I heard no sounds until I was a few yards from the door that opened into the lobby behind the registration desk. Then I heard voices just beyond the heavy door. I opened it a crack. My clerk, Sam Shurk, stood behind the desk with his back to me. Across the desk Peter Jellicoe talked earnestly. I tried to hear, but there was too much other noise in the narrow lobby on a cold wet afternoon that drove the derelict lonely back inside. And even as I watched, Jellicoe left the desk to climb the stairs and vanish through the second-floor door.

"Sam!"

Shurk looked up and all around the seedy lobby where the shabby and aimless tenants were restlessly dozing, furtively drinking or snarling in loud arguments about the events of the day with the vicious certainty of those who know nothing of what is going on beyond their own narrow world.

"Behind you, damn it!"

Shurk whirled and saw my face at the crack in the doorway. He suddenly smiled eagerly. The game was afoot! He came back, glanced behind to be sure we weren't seen and closed the door behind him. He stood in the dim back corridor.

"Mr. Shaw! This guy was just here asking questions! I was gonna call you and that detective Karnes, but you first because. . . ."

"Start from the beginning. He came in a few minutes ago."

Sam nodded. "Yeah, well, he came in, and I spotted him for a real stranger right off. I mean, he looked at the lobby like he never knew there was anythin' like it in the whole world. Anyway, he comes slow up to the desk and right off shows me this snapshot and asks me if the guy'd come into the hotel a lot. I told him, as far as I know, he never come in, I never saw him."

"What was the man's name?"

"He didn't say."

"What did the man look like? In the snapshot?"

Shurk shrugged. "Like a lot of guys, you know? Skinny, short hair, suit and tie, kind of messy. Thin face, hair maybe brown or maybe gray, it wasn't no color shot."

"Short or tall?"

"Couldn't tell. Thin guys always look tall on their own."

"Go on."

"Well, then he said maybe the guy'd come in with that Garou kid and his mother or maybe with Luis Marquez, and I'd just sort of forgotten."

"Had you?"

He shook his head. "No way, Mr. Shaw. Like I told the cops and this guy, I never even saw that Marquez in here before last night, and I never saw no one with the Garous."

"What else did he want?"

"That's all. Except he asked what room the Garous had been in. I told him, and I told him the cops had it sealed up, but he went on up anyway."

"All right," I said. "When he comes down, if he does anything except walk out, come to the front and signal me, okay? I'm in the alley across the street."

I put another ten into his hand. He grinned, so pleased to be working as a detective he almost refused it. Almost.

"Thanks, Mr. Shaw. I'll keep real good watch."

I left the way I had come, crossed back over the street to my Ferrari. A wino stood at the car, filthy rag in his scarred hand. "Clean the windshield, mister? One quarter, okay?" I gave him fifty cents, he'd had the intelligence not to put his rag on the windshield before I returned.

"Never mind the windshield," I said.

Peter Jellicoe came out of the Grace Hotel a few minutes later. He'd had no time to do much but walk straight out, and I got no sign from Sam Shurk. Jellicoe went straight to his Porsche, angrily chased off the same wino and his dirty rag, and drove out of the littered lot.

———— **Ten** ————

I TAILED PETER JELLICOE through the clearing afternoon and the falling temperature. To a French restaurant in the mid-Twenties off Fifth Avenue—Le Renard. It was long past lunchtime and not yet really cocktail time, but the restaurant seemed open. I gave Jellicoe a couple of minutes, then went in after him.

The restaurant had a low ceiling that made me duck as I came in down a step. There were three rooms, opening right, left and straight ahead, and a small bar directly inside the entrance. One lone man sat at the bar, but all three eating rooms seemed to be empty. At the in-between hour the checkroom was closed, the barman was checking his supplies for the night ahead, and a solitary waiter sat sipping a Coke at a table in the bar area. I sat at the bar, ordered a beer and looked around. The beer was bottled, imported only, and expensive. Then I saw Peter Jellicoe at a table in the far front corner of the room to the right. He wasn't alone. Estelle Jellicoe was talking earnestly to him.

I could see them from the bar through a lattice and some hanging plants. They had not seen me as far as I could tell. I drank my overpriced beer. They were the only patrons in the room and probably in the restaurant at this hour, but the lone waiter didn't seem annoyed, so I guessed that one or both of them was a habitué of the place. I was considering how I could get closer to them to try to hear what they were talking about when Peter got up abruptly and came toward the bar. I turned my back fast, became very interested in my beer. I didn't have to. Jellicoe went straight out of the restaurant without even glancing toward the bar. I finished my beer. The big adman didn't return. In the other room Estelle Jellicoe waved to the solitary waiter. He took her another martini.

Reluctantly I ordered another beer, picked up the bottle and the glass, and went to join her. She looked up at me as I sat down at her table but said nothing. She'd been at the table a long time. The debris of her lunch was still on the cloth, the ashtray was full, and five olive spears from martinis were neatly lined up in front of her as if she were keeping score. As I sat, she slowly rearranged the spears to point toward me, added the sixth spear. She still wore the tailored blue tweed skirt and jacket, pale blue blouse and navy high heels she'd had on when she'd come into her son's office earlier. But now she'd kicked the shoes off, sat relaxed with her elbow hooked over the back of her chair and her head resting against the wall behind her.

"Long lunch," I said.

"They know me in here," Estelle Jellicoe said. She drank her martini. "I often have long lunches, Mr. Shaw, especially the liquid part. It helps me forget how little I have to do."

"What do you want to do?"

"Almost anything," she said. "That is, anything that isn't considered to be woman's work. How is the snooping going?"

"Slowly," I said. "You don't like being a woman?"

"I love being a woman. I don't like what society tries to make a woman do and be." She lighted a cigarette. "You didn't come here to socialize."

"What did Peter want at El Jazz Latino and the Grace Hotel?"

"I wouldn't know." She drank. "What makes you think he was at those places?"

"I saw him. At both places."

"Seems an odd way to run an advertising agency, doesn't it?"

"You don't know what he was looking for?"

"I don't know that he was looking for anything, and I'm not sure I especially care."

She had been drinking most of the afternoon, slowly from the look of it, but steadily, and she was a shade drunk. Not a lot, but enough to bring a change over her. As if she had taken on a different shape and not for the worse. Calmer, easier, loose and relaxed in the empty restaurant with the stress and push of the city somehow distant.

"He's showing the snapshot of some man," I said.

"Why not?" she said. She drank, smoked, closed her eyes with her head back against the wall.

"Who is it?" I said. "Matt Jurgens?"

She didn't open her eyes. "Yes."

"Why? Not to find the murderer."

She opened her eyes, dropped her arm from the back of the chair, leaned toward me. "We have a right to know what Matt was doing! What he was doing instead of tending to the agency. We have a right to know what that fifty thousand was for."

"And what happened to it?" I said.

She sat back again. "That, too."

"What had Peter found out?"

"Not a damn thing. As dumb as his father, damn it. He learned nothing, and he let you spot him. Not very bright."

She finished her martini and waved to her private waiter. He still didn't seem at all annoyed. She probably tipped more than generously. I nursed my second beer. The waiter sneered but left. She smoked while we waited for her martini, seemed to be watching something fascinating on the wall behind me or a lot farther away than that. Something dark about her now, intense and brooding.

"You asked me what I wanted to do," she said. "I want to do what I'm capable of doing, what I have the intelligence to do. No one is going to let me. It's too late. I could run the agency, almost any business that doesn't require a special skill, but I don't have the record, the training, the credentials. Because I was a girl. I was trained to be a woman, no one ever even thinking I might want to do more—or at least something else. I had two brothers. They were taught, trained, aimed and helped toward business, careers, earning potential. Do you have any idea what it's like for a bright, capable girl to see her dumber brothers being pushed ahead? What it's like for a woman to watch her husband and son doing work she knows she can do better? Work they aren't any damn good at and don't really even want to do?"

"You'd like to run the agency yourself," I said.

"You bet I would," she said. "And could. Better than Matt or Bill or any of them."

"Better than Peter?"

The waiter came with her drink. She stirred the martini, ate the olive, arranged the spear in the row with the others.

"Or is Peter running it the same thing as you running it?" I said. "You'll run the show through him."

She shrugged, leaned back again, her head against the wall and her eyes watching me.

"You're sure you don't already know what Matt was doing?" I said. "Outside the agency? Or that maybe he wasn't doing anything at all? Peter's after something else, maybe making sure the wrong tracks aren't found?"

She went on watching me. "You think we killed Matt?"

"It's a possibility."

"So we could take control of the agency? Or I could."

"It's a motive."

She drank. "You're a good-looking man. Married?"

"Yes," I said. "Fifty thousand dollars is a motive, too. Especially if Matt Jurgens never had it."

"And too young for me," she said.

"You're not that old," I said. "Is being the power behind the throne going to be enough? Operating the agency through Peter?"

"At my age," she said, "it's all I have."

"If Sarah Jurgens lets you have it."

"Yes," she said. She finished her martini, continued to watch me. "Take a little tip about our Sarah. She's not all she seems. In her own way she's a very tough cookie. Or have you figured that out by now?"

"Tough in what way?" I said.

"A female way," Estelle Jellicoe said, scorn now in the dark voice. "She gets what she wants, and she uses men to help her get what she wants. She used Matt and she'll use you."

"How did she use Matt?"

She ran her fingers slowly around inside the rim of her martini glass. She licked the finger. "I don't know exactly, but I know the way they lived was her way. I know that Matt hadn't been happy for years. Not at home, not at the office."

''Not even at his own agency?''

She shook her head. ''Matt never really wanted to be a businessman.''

''But you want to,'' I said. ''You've wanted to run a business for a long time. You feel you're good at it, should be doing it. You've felt that for a long time.''

''Yes,'' she said. She stubbed out her cigarette, stood up. ''Ladies' room.''

I watched her walk through the bar and turn left around a corner out of my sight. Suddenly I liked her a lot more than I had. It's not easy for a bright woman in this world today and never for a bright woman tied to not-too-bright men. She has to spend half her life acting, pretending. For their sake more than for hers. Sometimes watching them botch her life as well as their own.

I was still thinking about this after the waiter had come with the bill for my pair of beers. As he left with the cash, I saw that he was in street clothes as if his day was over and he was going home. I got up and headed back through the bar to the ladies' room. Its door was open. It was being cleaned. And it was empty.

It turned out that Le Renard had a rear entrance that opened onto a commercial parking lot where they had the cars stacked two high on metal racks. Estelle Jellicoe wasn't in the lot. Not anymore. I went around in front to my own car. She wasn't on the street, either, and neither was Peter Jellicoe's Porsche.

In the clearing and chilling evening I stood feeling the temperature plunge toward true winter, watching a thin sun angling down the narrow canyons of the city from over New Jersey across the river. She'd fooled me, given me the slip. Why? There could be a hundred reasons from the sudden need to sleep off an afternoon of martinis to a panic because she *had* killed Matt Jurgens.

It had been a long day. I decided to think it all over in the sauna, pool and dining room of my athletic club up-town on West Fifty-sixth Street. I fell asleep in the heat of the sauna, did twenty laps in the almost empty pool and had a first-rate quiche Alsace and veal *romano* with as-paragus in the dining room. By the time I reached the Sacher torte and coffee, I still had the same hundred-odd possible reasons for the actions of both Jellicoes, a lot of dead ends and the silent man out in the Melvilles' semi-detached in Brooklyn.

I had three cups of coffee and a small cognac. Then I went down to the club garage, reclaimed my Ferrari and drove out to the West Side Highway and the Battery Tun-nel and Brooklyn again. Dark now, the first heavy chill of winter hanging over the shine of the Narrows and Brook-lyn itself.

Eleven

THERE WAS LIGHT in the semidetached with its brown grass and empty flower beds on the side street six blocks from the dark water of the bay. The blue Datsun wasn't in the driveway. No car was, yet shadows moved behind the drawn shades of the house, and all up and down the dark street cars were parked and people trooped in and out of the Melville house.

I pulled into the driveway of a house without lights across the street, lighted a cigarette and sat watching. The people going in and out of the semidetached were all kinds: old people and young couples; businessmen in suits and ties and youths with long hair and beards; girls in jeans and club women; laborers in work clothes and fishermen still wearing rubber boots; firemen and policemen in uniform. I watched for over two hours before the flow of people began to slacken.

It was into the second hour that the battered blue Datsun drove up again. It turned into the driveway as before, parked, and the short, burly man with the bull neck and close-cropped hair got out once more. Or I thought it was the same man. For a moment I wasn't sure, something very different about him now. He wore a suit, shabby and unpressed, a narrow tie and a white shirt with its collar curled, carried a worn gray hat and seemed somehow smaller as he smiled nervously at the people going in and out of the house, hesitant, almost humble. Then he walked toward the rear again, and the oddly quick, gliding walk was still there, soft and soundless for such a heavy man.

I watched him until he disappeared behind the house.

Soon the flow of visitors began to dwindle, more leaving the house than arriving, the cars slowly becoming fewer on the quiet Brooklyn street. After another half hour there were only three cars left, a few last shadows standing on the glassed-in porch saying their farewells to whoever was inside the house. I pinched out my cigarette and waited. The last cars left, and there was only the blue Datsun in the driveway.

I got out and strolled to the corner like any home owner out to get some air before bed. I wished I'd stopped at the penthouse to pick up a coat, the light raincoat didn't hold out the sudden winter cold at all. At the corner I crossed the street and began to walk back toward the Melville house. The lights were still on in the neglected semide-tached, but I saw no shadows now on the drawn blinds. There was no light in the house on this side, and I circled around it to come up on my quarry from the back.

I reached the driveway for the other half of the Melville semi and dropped to the ground.

Someone else was watching the Melvilles.

Two of them. One in the shelter of a corner of the Melville garage. Another crouched behind the car in this driveway where he could watch the front of the house. In the dark I could see only their outlines, vague and indistinct. They didn't seem to have seen me, and I crawled backward away from the driveway until I was in the deep shadow of the next house.

There was no way I could get close to the man behind the car in the driveway, but with a little luck I might be able to circle through the backyard of the house facing the next block and get near enough to the figure at the Melville garage to see who it was. I crawled to the back fence, slipped over, circled around the two attached garages and came up to the front corner of the garage behind the Melville half of the house. The shadowy figure crouched a few feet away.

Two other shadows stood behind me.

"Hey, *hombre,* funny man."

The hard rod poked into my back once again.

"Hey, make a joke, funny man."

A half turn told me it was the swarthy driver with the drooping black mustache who had driven me from the Grace Hotel to dump me under the West Side Highway. The gun in his hand was real. The man with him was small and thin, dark-skinned and silent. He had a gun, too. So did the one who had been watching the house from the shadow of the garage, I felt it against my arm from behind me.

"Take him," the third voice said. The mezzo-soprano who had been in the back seat the first time they had taken me.

"Hey, *amigo,* you hear? We gonna take 'nother li'l trip."

It was a long drive this time. That was all right with me. Across Brooklyn and Queens to the Triborough Bridge, the driver whistling off-key all the way, the small thin Latin and a twin on either side of me. The mezzo woman was not with us. We were not in the red Oldsmobile Cutlass. But I had a hunch that the Olds wasn't far away, and that the woman was in it.

All the way to the Triborough Bridge and across into
Manhattan. East Harlem and driving south and west
through the dark and dirty streets strewn with the litter of
the poor and forgotten, the ignored, the exploited. To the
rubble of an empty lot among the black tenements where
laundry hung high and ghostly from the buildings to the
backyard poles. East Harlem where I would not have many
friends.

The steel door in the side of one of the black brick
buildings clanged shut behind us. The dimly lighted corridor echoed hollow and empty as I walked between my
captors. Into a silent empty apartment and a bare kitchen.
The skinny pair pushed me into a straight chair, tied my
hands behind me and my legs to the rungs, and sat me
facing a chipped white enamel table. The driver brought
a floor lamp and set it to shine directly into my face. An
empty chair was placed facing me on the other side of the
chipped table. My attendants stepped back, hovering like
ghosts just beyond the edge of light. They'd all seen too
many international spy movies.

"The late show," I said. "Where're your Gestapo uni-
forms?"

The mustachioed driver came from behind the light. He
bent across the chipped table. He slapped my face. From
the glitter of his black eyes he'd wanted to do that for a
long time.

"You too damn funny, you know, man?"

The voice came from behind the light.

"Did I say to hit him, Rafael?"

"Funny gringo," the driver said.

I saw movement behind the light. There was a stirring.
The mezzo emerged beside the swarthy driver. She said
something in Spanish. The driver, Rafael, faded into the
thick black beyond the light. The woman sat down facing

me across the table. She was small, dark eyed and dark haired. A slim nose and pale coffee-colored skin. Long hair that half hid her face. I realized now that she was the unknown third person I had seen at the bar in El Jazz Latino earlier this afternoon. The one who had asked a lot of questions about the man in Brooklyn. She asked more questions.

"You are a detective?"

"Private," I said.

"You work for the wife?"

"What wife?"

She sat, one leg crossed over the other, the crossed leg swinging up and down, up and down. A nice leg. Two nice legs under a slim skirt. She spoke slowly in that mezzo-soprano voice, low and flat. A good-looking woman. Beautiful now that I thought about it. It grew on you, her beauty, the way her voice did. Rich and low, her voice in the dim room, but a monotone now, hypnotic. The slim leg swinging, swinging.

"The wife of Matt Jurgens."

"Yes."

"To do what for her?"

"Find out who killed her husband."

"That is all?"

"Find out why."

Her leg swung up and down, up and down, in the bare room somewhere in East Harlem, and I suddenly knew that she, or they, had been involved with Matt Jurgens. I had known from the first time I saw the red Olds in Douglaston that they had some connection to the killing, but now I sensed that they had known Matt Jurgens *before* his death. That somehow they were a part of his murder.

"Who are these Garou people?"

"I thought maybe you could tell me."

"We do not know them. Who are they?"

"I told you. People from New Orleans. She was a go-go dancer once. There's some connection between them and Matt Jurgens around 1966. That guy in Brooklyn could be mixed up with them."

"What is it Peter Jellicoe does now? His mother?"

"They want to take over the agency."

"He would kill to do that? The mother?"

"Maybe."

"Now they will get the agency?"

"I don't think so."

"Why not?"

"Sarah Jurgens won't let them."

"She can stop them?"

"She owns the company now."

"So?"

It was a small word, but it carried a lot of weight in the empty room. A heavy weight right on Sarah Jurgens. When someone is murdered, look for who profits the most. I'd thought about that, but it looked like Sarah Jurgens had lost the most, too. They seemed to have different ideas. The slim mezzo went into a long discussion in fast Spanish with her unseen buddies behind the light. Something seemed to have them interested. I had a few questions of my own. How had they known Matt Jurgens before his murder? Where did they fit? I waited for the Spanish to cool down, for the mezzo to turn back to me, and took a shot at getting an answer.

"What did Matt Jurgens really do on his business trips? I mean, besides his agency work?"

A shot in the dark, but so far it was the only place where I could fit them into the picture. I got a reaction. Not the one I wanted. Silence. Sudden coldness in the dark eyes of the mezzo in the slim skirt. Some Spanish. My ropes checked by my two diminutive attendants. Some more Spanish. Then the light went out. I sat in the dark.

"Well," I said, "I can always use some rest."

No one answered. No one moved. A door closed somewhere in the distance. They'd walked out and left me tied up in the dark like a chicken waiting for the ax.

"Hey!"

There was no answer. I was alone in the dark room. Then I wasn't.

No more than a weight in the darkness. A movement of the silent room. Something. There in the emptiness.

A sound. Perhaps a step. And another.

I remembered a small man inside the oval opening of the gas chamber waiting for death. Strapped in his chair, empty eyed, helpless. The prisoner in a French movie, lashed quickly hand and foot and dragged to the flat board to be pushed under the dropping blade of the guillotine. The staked chicken waiting for the teeth of the tiger.

Behind me in the blackness of the barren room there was someone. Something. A mass in the silence. As if some monster from beneath the city breathed in the blackness and the silence.

The muzzle of a gun pressed lightly against my head. Just enough to be there. A hand began to search me. A thick hand in my pockets, against my shirt, along my belt and pants. A hand that took my wallet, my change, the photo of the Garou woman, the flyer, my address book and my small notebook. Touched my shoulder harness, but the Latins had already removed my gun.

The hand went away. I sat stripped. The gun did not go away. Faintly the gun pressed harder. The hammer cocked.

I thought then of nothing at all. How long I didn't know. My mind empty. Nothing moved anywhere. Not in the world. A world without movement. Without color. Without time. . . .

The gun was gone.

I listened to the dark room. The slum building beyond the apartment. The littered Harlem night far off.

Somewhere there were more sounds, noises. A door. A cat in the debris of the night. A car fading away. Footsteps again. I waited for the gun. For the end of time. The weight in the room again, the movement of air behind me.

"Who are you?"

I sensed a change, a difference.

"Who was the other man in here?"

No gun against my head. Only a voice, talking to me.

"The one who just ran out?"

My voice would not come.

"You hurt?"

I shook my head. Tried to shake my head. Nothing moved. A hand felt the pulse of my neck.

"Scared. You'll be okay. Try to talk."

I managed a nod.

"Who was the other guy?"

"Don't know." My voice! A voice I barely knew.

"Was it Garou?"

"The boy? No."

He seemed to think somewhere behind me in the dark room.

"Who are you?"

"Shaw," I said. Tried again. "Paul Shaw. Thayer, Shaw and Delaney, Investigators."

"Let's see the license."

"He took it. The other man. He took everything. Except the gun. They took that. The Latins."

"What are you doing here?"

"Working on a case."

"What case?"

"Murder of a man named Matt Jurgens."

"What do those Hispanic types have to do with the murder?"

"I don't know."

"Who are they? What did they want with you?"

"I'm not sure. I think one of their friends was killed, too. But I'm pretty sure they were mixed up with Jurgens before all this. And later Luis Marquez was killed in the Garous' room."

"The Garous' room?"

"At the Grace Hotel down in the Bowery."

"So?" He thought about something again. "How do the Garous tie in with both your murder and those Puerto Ricans?"

"That's a big damn question. I haven't seen the boy or his mother since yesterday at the Grace Hotel."

I could feel him watching me, staring at my neck somewhere back there in the silent room. Then a knife touched cold on my wrists, cut the ropes holding my hands. I turned to look at him. He was already walking away. A tall, thin man with stooped shoulders, framed in the doorway of the apartment by the weak light of the corridor.

"What's your part in all this?" I said.

He didn't answer. Didn't even turn. He went out, closed the door leaving me in darkness to untie my own feet. I untied them in a hurry. Two strangers in the darkness was enough. And how did I know that the first one wouldn't come back? With his cocked pistol.

Free, I got out of there. Out of the room, the empty apartment, the long and deserted corridor with its feeble light and slum smell of damp and rot and stale food. Into the open night.

I stood breathing deeply but not feeling a lot safer. It

was still East Harlem, and I was alone. I'd learned a long time ago in another ghetto that strangers are rarely welcome or safe, and for mostly good reasons. The poor and ethnic minorities have learned to expect little good from Anglo strangers. Shaky and nervous, I looked for the shortest way to a major avenue and saw my little Ferrari.

It was parked in the open area next to the dark building. They had taken my keys and driven it here from Brooklyn. It was unlocked, the keys were still in it, and it was undamaged. That said a lot for the power of my Latin friends, at least on this particular block.

I asked no more silent questions. I drove out of the debris of the empty lot, out of the back streets, out of East Harlem and downtown to my office and the cocktail lounge on the side street that was my favorite bar.

Twelve

I NEEDED THE first two Scotches. The third I began to enjoy. I knew that death had been close to me tonight. Closer than I'd ever sensed it even back in Nam. I didn't know who the second man in that East Harlem room had been, the one who'd finally cut me loose, but I knew somehow that the first one, the one who had cocked the gun against my head, had been a killer.

I enjoyed the third Scotch all the way, then went up to our office to call Maureen. I was feeling scared and mortal, and I wanted a soft ear to tell it to. After 11:00 P.M. our empty corridor looked more than ever like an Egyptian tomb—smooth, silent, windowless, lighted by some invisible source and all doors identical. Phoning from my private office, I got the production-company field operator, who told me that Miss Shaw was wrapping up the last scene of the day and would get back to me.

While I waited, I got my spare Colt out of the safe, a new checkbook, some money out of petty cash, a duplicate of my license and driver's license, and left instructions for one of our Finns to report the losses of the licenses and credit cards. I needed official replacements for the licenses, and I had the strong hunch that the credit cards would be used, so I wanted the action fast.

Maureen called back. "Paul? It's late back there."

She was worried. I told her about the room in East Harlem. That really worried her. "Oh, Paul, it's all so awful!"

"I'm alive," I said.

"By chance! A hair! How can we live like this?"

"It's my work, Maurie. I'll be all right."

We talked a while longer, nothing special, then said we loved each other and hung up. Being a movie actress is hard work, she was as tired as I was. Maybe more. I'd got it off my chest, the fear and the helplessness, passed some of it on to her and now felt a lot better. We use people more than we know. And other people use us.

The violent knocking on my outer-office door broke me out of the reverie. Also out of my better feelings. I gripped my new Colt and crossed the dark outer office to the front door.

"Yes?"

The knocking got louder.

"Paul? Is that you? Open the door! Quick! Please!"

Sarah Jurgens. I opened the door. She came in past me, her face frantic and her eyes scared. A red dress, cut low at the breasts and tight at the hips, under an open mink coat.

"Someone's following me! He wants to kill me, too! I know he wants to kill me!"

I leaned out and looked along our antiseptic corridor. I saw no one and heard nothing except the elevator going back down. It's an automatic; the only attendant in the building nights and weekends is the doorman-guard in the lobby. He has strict instructions to let in anyone who asks to see us. As Thayer says, "In our business you don't make appointments. When people want us, sometimes they're in a hurry. It's a risk we take.''

But if anyone had followed Sarah into the building, he wasn't in sight. I closed the door. Even in the dimness of our outer office I could see she was shivering.

"Why, Paul? Why would he want to kill me, too?''

I guided her into my private office, sat her down in one of my chrome-and-soft-leather Swedish armchairs. She stared at my face the whole time. I sat on the matching ottoman, watched her distraught face under the blond hair.

"Who followed you, Sarah?''

She shook her head, back and forth, over and over. "A man. I came in on the Long Island to talk to you, maybe have dinner. I've been alone all day. I don't like to be alone. I had to be with someone, Paul, with you. Some dinner. A little wine. Someone to talk to me. Perhaps forget death and greed and hate. Then I saw him following me!''

"From Douglaston?''

"How do I know? I saw him first at Penn Station. I mean, I know I saw him at the station, but I didn't know he was following me then. On the way here in my taxi I realized that another cab was behind us all the way from the station. When I saw him get out of the cab in front of your building, I remembered seeing him at Penn.''

"What does he look like?''

"No,'' she said, rocked. "I don't know. A dark coat, a dark hat pulled down. A big man, I think. I never saw his face. A mustache maybe, dark glasses. He was hunched over. I tried to go around the block and lose him, but he was still behind me when I ran into the building and came up. I know he's waiting out there. He wants to kill me, Paul! Why?''

"Yes," I said, "why? Why would anyone follow you, want to kill you?"

"Don't say it like that! It terrifies me."

"What do you know, Sarah? What do you know that you haven't told me?"

"Nothing!"

"What do you have you forgot to tell me about?"

"Nothing, Paul! I swear! Oh, you don't believe me!"

"What was Matt's connection to those Latins?"

"He had none! He never knew people like that!"

"What was he really doing with that Garou boy and his go-go mother?"

"Nothing! Why are you doing this, Paul? I can't stand all these questions!"

"What was he doing that wasn't agency business?"

"Nothing! Nothing! Nothing!"

She clamped her hands over her ears and rocked her head back and forth again. Stared at me and beyond me to my high windows over the dark city with its endless lights. I took her wrists gently and pulled her hands from her ears as she watched my face half in fear and half in hope, anticipation in her bright eyes. Maybe she liked her men rough.

"Something," I said softly. "Matt was doing something. Perhaps with the Garous, perhaps with those Puerto Ricans or whatever they all are, perhaps with someone we don't even know, perhaps alone. But he was doing something more than his work for the agency, and he had been for a long time."

She watched me, shook her head, "No, Paul. I don't know. Oh, you've got to believe me, Paul! I'm all alone now. You've got to help me."

"I am helping you," I said. I still held her wrists, tried to force her to keep looking at me. "Sarah, Matt took fifty thousand dollars from the agency office. Apparently in cash. He just took it out, gave no reason. Where is it, Sarah? Did he bring it home? Is that what his murder was all about?''

I felt her stiff wrists go loose, the tension fading from them. Her quick eyes calmed as if I'd slapped her face. Sharp eyes, thinking now. Money was more than words, sobering to her.

''Fifty thousand?''

''That's what he took home. He had the right, but usually a boss says why he needs the money. He never said why. Why, Sarah?''

She took her hands away from me. ''I never knew that, Paul, I swear it. I never knew anything about it. Matt never said a word. I never saw any money.''

''He didn't talk about needing money for something? He said nothing about trouble involving money? No hint of what he was going to do with fifty thousand dollars?''

She stood up in the quiet office, the noise of the night city far below, and looked out at the view. A glitter of lights now on the slow river and across Brooklyn. ''I swear he said nothing about any money, Paul. I never saw any money, never knew it was in the house if it was. But it has to be the reason, doesn't it? It must have been a thief after all! Stole the money and killed Matt! It had to be someone who knew the money was there. That boy! Of course, it was blackmail! Some kind of blackmail! Matt got the money for the boy! I never heard him say anything about needing that much money for anything else, business or personal! That must be it, Paul!''

''You could be right.''

''I know I am! Now someone must think I knew about the money. Think I saw something.'' She shivered, turned

to look at me. "I need a drink. I'm scared, Paul. Take me
somewhere. Now. Take me anywhere we can get a drink."

"There's a bar around the corner," I said.

She took my arm, leaned her face against my shoulder
as we walked out into the long deserted corridor.

Over her second martini she leaned back in the booth and
closed her eyes.

"He never did talk to me about business. I suppose
that's why I never took much interest in the agency. Actually he never talked to me about much of anything after
the first few years."

Close to midnight, the small lounge was quiet. This was
midtown, the business district, and the bar did most of its
business in the afternoon and early evening. I had always
liked it at the later hours. They served a good steak sand-
wich, and quiet suited the narrow room with its red plush
and dark wood. Sarah Jurgens seemed to appreciate the
quiet, the muted glitter.

"You come in here often, Paul?"

"Often enough," I said. "Hungry? They have a good
steak."

"Not really," she said, swirled the olive in her martini.
"We stopped talking so soon, Matt and I. I don't really
know why. At first we talked all the time. The early years.
About our plans, our hopes, our ideas. Then we stopped.
I don't know why or even exactly when. I remember I kept
trying to talk when he came home, on weekends when we
weren't busy with parties or something else. About the
agency, his work, the house we were planning, vacations,
our friends, everything. It didn't seem to do any good.
Somehow we just stopped talking."

There were only three other late drinkers in the hush of
the lounge. A young couple still talking a lot to each other

and a small middle-aged man who seemed to be waiting for something or someone he didn't really expect to come. Neither of those fitted the description of the man Sarah had seen following her. There was a single long window at the front more than half-covered by a thick velvet curtain. I had my eye toward it, but no one had looked in yet. She talked on as she drank.

"So much pure chance is involved in any marriage, in just falling in love. All marriages, good or bad. I had a man years ago I know now was the one I should have married. He was exactly right for me, what I needed. But I was in love with someone else at the time, you know? The one I was in love with was all wrong for me, but at the time I couldn't see that, I wanted only him. Isn't that the way it always happens? Pure chance. In the end I lost both of them and ended up with Matt."

A short man came in with a tall woman. Were they right for each other? Did they care? He seemed nervous, belligerent, as if every tall man tried to take her from him. Perhaps that was what he needed. Perhaps she needed to have tall men try to take her, as long as they failed. They couldn't be following Sarah. If anyone really was.

"He was a good man, Paul. A good husband, but so dull. We never really had a lot in common. He did everything a husband is supposed to do, gave me a home, support, security. But that was all, after the first few years anyway. All work and business. I like to play, live high, go places, travel. He buried me out there in Douglaston! After the first years we never went out. Not even when he was home. Away all the time, month after month! Leaving me alone! In that cemetery of a suburb!"

She was moving from sadness to anger. Maybe it was the martinis on an empty stomach. Dredging up the past and an edge coming into her voice as she relived her years with the dead Matt Jurgens, a hard edge, bitter. Restless, she drained her martini, smiled at me. I ordered another martini and my Scotch.

"Most people," I said, watched the waiter and the door where no one had come in for some time, "I think most people marry the right person for them whether they know it or not. Whether they let themselves admit it or not."

The drinks came. No one had stopped outside the front window to look in at us since we had arrived.

"What we think we need is just delusion?" She stirred the martini with her finger, sucked the finger. "What counts is what we do? Who we actually marry? And we marry the same person over and over, don't we? Maybe we never know what we really want, what the other person really wants. We never know anyone else at all. I never really knew Matt, and now he's gone. I don't have a husband. I don't have children. I don't even have friends. Just a house I hate, money and a company. Well, maybe I'll travel. I can go anywhere I want to. With anyone I want to. Or I could run the agency. That might be fun."

"The Jellicoes will love you."

"The hell with Estelle! And Junior! That could be the best part! Make them both crawl. To me!"

"Is that what you want?"

She shrugged. "I don't know."

"You'd better find out."

She drank. "Oh, hell, maybe I'll just let Harry Glanz run the whole show. He always wanted to be top dog. Throw Junior a bone, second-in-command, make Estelle happy. I don't care about the damned company or the money! I want to live, move, enjoy life. I want to make love. Now. I've tried every trick to lure you into bed, now I'm tired of that. Take me somewhere. Anywhere we can make love. Now!"

I'm not immune. Maureen was two thousand miles away. We have a modern marriage, if there really is such a thing, and Maureen was in Arizona. I paid the check. Under the circumstances I wouldn't be able to put it on Sarah's bill. We took my Ferrari. To the Drake Hotel. Maureen wouldn't want me to take her to our penthouse, our marriage wasn't that modern. She, Sarah, held my arm in both hands all the way, her head pressed against my shoulder, not looking at anything.

Maybe Maureen had been away too long. I was excited. That was the only reason I would have missed the taxi behind us until we got out at the Drake and started inside. I saw it then and saw the big man in the dark coat and hat reflected in the glass doors of the hotel as he slipped off into the shadows. At the desk I registered only Sarah. She opened her mouth.

"I spotted your tail," I said without looking at her, bent over the register. "He's outside now. You go up alone. I'll join you when I've got him pinned."

"Outside? Go up alone?" She was torn. She didn't want to go alone. She wanted sex. The need in her from her husband's death was tearing her up. But she was scared, too. The man outside could be the killer.

"All right. Catch him, Paul!" She watched me with the wide eyes of both fear and need. "Hurry."

Thirteen

I WALKED INTO the elevator with her, got off on the first floor, went down the fire stairs and peered out into the lobby. He already stood at the registration desk talking hard to the desk clerk. With the overcoat buttoned to his chin and his low hat, dark glasses and fake mustache, he looked ridiculous, and he had probably walked straight up to the hotel desk the moment we went up in the elevator. Totally unaware that he had been spotted hours ago. An amateur. Peter Jellicoe.

Talking to the desk clerk, Jellicoe was excited. Had seeing Sarah Jurgens and me going into a hotel excited him? Because if we'd been doing that before Matt Jurgens was murdered, maybe we'd killed Matt, and he'd get the agency after all? Or because our hanky-panky gave him someone else to try to blame for his own murder of Matt Jurgens? Or something else? Whatever, I was about to step across the lobby and put him out of his euphoria over his clever tailing when I saw the other man.

He sat quietly in a far corner of the lobby near the doors, reading the evening paper, sometimes dozing off with the paper in his lap. But he wasn't dozing and he wasn't reading. He was watching Peter Jellicoe, and maybe earlier me and Sarah Jurgens, and he was no amateur. He was the short, bull-necked, soft-moving and expressionless man from the Melville house in Brooklyn, and he knew what he was doing. He looked now like still another man, the work clothes and the shabby brown suit and stained shirt gone. Dressed in a new gray pinstripe with a light blue shirt and Madison Avenue rep tie, his close-cropped prisonlike haircut covered by a snappy gray hat with a bright band and a jaunty feather. As dapper as such a thick man could get, he seemed taller and slimmer this time. Not an amateur, no, whatever else he was.

He watched Peter Jellicoe, and he watched the elevators where Sarah and I had gone up, and he watched everything else in the hotel. The silent tiger in the jungle, missing nothing. Yet concentrating on Jellicoe and the elevators. Who was he tailing? Peter Jellicoe, Sarah or me? Or all of us? Began with one, found the others and interested in us all? His immersion in what he was doing, whether it was watching a TV alone in an empty semidetached in Brooklyn or watching a man in a busy Manhattan hotel, showed a single-mindedness that was almost chilling. I sensed a man who would never miss a chance to get something the easy way, who looked at the world only for what was in it for him, for what he could grab and take. Ruthless.

When Peter Jellicoe turned away from the hotel desk and walked back out into the October night, the man from Brooklyn shook out his topcoat, casually searched the pockets for something he wanted as he strolled after Jellicoe. I gave them a moment, then slipped out the fire-exit door into the dark street. In front of the hotel Peter Jellicoe was hailing a cab. The man from Brooklyn was nowhere I could see. My Ferrari was in the hotel garage, I'd have to hope for a taxi at the right time. Jellicoe got his cab. I didn't move out of the shadows of the hotel wall. I waited. The traffic was thick enough across town, the light ahead had just turned red, and I would have to risk losing Jellicoe anyway. I waited.

He appeared like a ghost from the dark across the midtown street as Jellicoe's taxi inched into the flow of traffic. Somehow he had managed to park the blue Datsun on the street. He was the kind of man who usually managed. But not everything. He had changed his clothes and his image but not his car. When the blue Datsun was far enough along the block, I came out of my shadows and slipped into a lucky top-lighted cab. The driver looked back.

"Just drive," I said.

He flipped down his flag, drove in silence. One of the sullen drivers. We reached the corner. The Datsun had turned south.

"Turn left."

Peter Jellicoe's cab was out of sight, but the silent man in the blue Datsun would not lose him. It was up to me not to lose the Datsun.

"Keep in the pack. Don't get hung by a light."

The traffic moved down the avenue in its phalanxlike pack, and after we crossed Forty-second Street, I was pretty sure where we were going. When the Datsun turned on Thirty-third, I knew. I could be wrong, but sometimes you have to take a chance to gain an edge in my business.

"Get to Penn Station as fast as you can."

He did. I was waiting in the paperback bookstore at the edge of the Long Island Railroad boarding area on the lower level when Peter Jellicoe arrived to join the other night travelers. He bought a ticket at the window. That told me he had almost certainly followed Sarah Jurgens all the way from Douglaston. Otherwise he would have driven into the city. Men who drive Porsches don't take commuter trains if they can help it.

I did not see the silent man from Brooklyn, but I knew he was there somewhere. Through the racks and the display window I watched Jellicoe buy his ticket, stop at an all-night stand for two hot dogs and an orange drink, and join the thin line of late commuters in front of the gate to the Port Washington train. He ate his frankfurters with the hunger of a large man who has missed his dinner and the satisfaction of someone who has had a good day. If I didn't pick up the beer-can crusher from the Melville house before the gates opened, I'd have a decision to make. I could take the train and tail Jellicoe—and I had a hunch he would lead me to mother, not wife—or brace him about Sarah Jurgens right on the train. Or I could try to find the man from the blue Datsun somewhere in the station. Jellicoe would keep, I knew where to find him. It was the silent man I really wanted now.

The gates opened at last, and Peter Jellicoe went down to his train with the other sleepy commuters. I left the bookstore. The thickset man came out of the drugstore three doors away. I ducked back. Had he seen me? He gave away nothing, moved on in that quick glide to the top of the stairs down to the Port Washington train and stared down as if to fix Peter Jellicoe and the train in his mind. Then he looked up for a time at the track board that listed the station stops. Then he walked away to the stairs up to Eighth Avenue. I had no chance of following him unseen through the narrow passage to that exit. I sprinted to the wide stairs up to the main level of the station and hurried to the Eighth Avenue exit.

He was halfway across the avenue, heading toward a narrow parking lot on Thirtieth Street. I trotted parallel on this side of Eighth. I saw the battered blue Datsun in the dim light of the half-empty parking lot, hailed a cruising cab and was waiting when he came toward me across the avenue going east on Thirtieth Street. My taxi moved ahead of him across town until he signaled a right turn on Second Avenue. I told the cabbie to turn with him and slowly drop back until we were behind the Datsun heading south. Down to Houston Street, and then south of Houston to Clinton Street and the Grace Hotel.

He parked across the street from the shabby hotel. I went on to the next corner, turned, paid off the cabbie and walked back. He was in front of the hotel. As I watched, he seemed to float to the dark opening of the alley that led around the Grace to the rear entrance and vanished.

I crossed Clinton with its last few staggering derelicts and furtive shadows waiting for easy prey and approached the alley slowly. Because I suddenly knew where else I had encountered the thick, silent man—in the dark room in East Harlem earlier tonight. He was the shadow who had expertly stripped me, silent and unseen, and had cocked his pistol against my head. Who must have followed me or the Latins from Brooklyn, and who knew all about me now. Who—whatever else he was—I knew, felt, sensed, was a killer.

I stood waiting in an empty doorway where I could watch the dark alley entrance. It was there like a black pit waiting for some unwary victim. I felt that if I stepped into it, I would cross into a different universe, an alien world of monsters without a name and terrors unknown in the world of reality.

From time to time a wandering drunk moved along the empty skid-row street. Somewhere near, someone coughed his lungs away and someone screamed. Someone laughed and someone cried. The endless sounds of the skid-row

night. The distant grunt of an unseen victim struggling to
keep his bottle or his money. The curses of the drunk-
roller meeting resistance. The small feet of rats running.

The man from Brooklyn did not come out of the alley
or the front entrance of the flophouse hotel. What did he
want here? I wouldn't find out in a doorway, watching an
alley entrance. I didn't want to cross the invisible line and
go into the alley after him, but I would have to. I gave
him ten more minutes. He did not appear. I took out my
small Colt and walked into the alley.

I moved warily up the alley toward the rear entrance of
the Grace. I had been here before, but somehow it was
different this time. I felt danger in every inch, the touch
of death. As if the thick, silent man from Brooklyn exuded
a sense of death like an executioner, a mass murderer.
Even the dark air seemed to have the touch of fear. I felt
the sweat running under my shirt in spite of the cold October night air, wiped my hands on my pants, gripped the
pistol tighter as I walked on. But the alley was empty. At
last I stood outside the rear door of the hotel. It was unlocked as usual.

Inside I stood with my back tight against the door and
scanned every inch of the long dim corridor. There was
no movement, and the only sounds were far ahead out in
the hotel lobby. At every narrow cross corridor in the maze
behind the registration desk of the ancient hotel I stopped
to scrutinize its length, my Colt alert. There was nothing,
and I reached the door into the lobby behind the registration desk. I opened it a crack. Sam Shurk slept in his chair
behind the desk. Two ragged derelicts sprawled asleep on
the shabby couches of the lobby. One old man sat erect in
a lobby chair, doing nothing, his eyes open and streaming
tears down onto his dirty tie.

The man from Brooklyn was nowhere in the lobby.

Where was he? He hadn't come out of the alley or the front entrance while I was watching. Unless I had just missed him going out the front while I came in the back, he was still in the hotel. I slipped through the door, holstering my pistol, and crossed the lobby without waking up Shurk or the derelicts. The crying old man didn't notice me. At the front entrance the Datsun was still across the street. There was nowhere to hide in the bare lobby, and I had seen and heard nothing in the dim corridors behind the reception desk.

I had a flash of memory and a hunch. The flash of a black-haired arm that reach out of room 27 on the third floor and dragged the boy, Ted Garou, inside. A hunch that sent me up the stairs, through the door to the second floor and on up to the third floor. I came out into the third-floor corridor cautiously, my gun out. Along the corridor there was light from an open door. It was room 27. I watched, waited and listened. For five minutes. There was neither sound nor movement inside room 27, no shadows crossed the light from the open doorway. I stepped softly along the corridor. The police seal on the door had been broken. I pushed the door open slowly, saw nothing in the room. Jumped into the room, gun in both hands, aimed at the part of the room I couldn't see from outside. The room was empty. The bathroom and closets were empty. But the room had been searched. Violently. What little there was to search.

A bare room of empty closets and empty drawers, but all the furniture had been moved, all the drawers pulled out and flung aside, all the doors and cabinets opened. My hunch told me that the man from the semidetached in Brooklyn, the man who had followed me or the Latins to Harlem and was now following everyone, was the man who had been in this room with Ted Garou and his mother the night Luis Marquez was killed. If he was, what was he doing back, and what was he looking for?

And where was he now?

He hadn't been in the lobby. He hadn't passed me going down as I came up. So there had to be another way down. I found it at the far end of the corridor—a door with a broken lock that opened onto back stairs. They looked as though they hadn't been used for years, yet the man had known they were there. A careful man who guarded his back. The stairs ended on the ground floor at a door that had been padlocked. The padlock had been broken. Recently. The door opened into the narrow corridors behind the registration desk. Silent and empty corridors.

I went back out to the lobby. Sam Shurk was gone from the desk, and my man wasn't in the lobby. At the front entrance the blue Datsun was gone from across the street. I'd lost him. The two derelicts still sprawled asleep on the shabby couches, the old man still sat stiffly in his chair, slow tears still in his blank eyes.

"Where's the desk clerk?" I said.

The derelicts slept on, oblivious. The old man cried his slow tears. I bent down to the old man.

"Where's Sam? The desk clerk. He was here."

After a moment the old man twitched, blinked up at me as if he had just seen me. He smiled almost happily. I was talking to him.

"Sam was here, sure was. Nice, Sam is. You know I had a house once? Sure did. Big house. Somewhere."

"Where did Sam go?"

The old man blinked. "Sam? He's at the desk."

"He was. He's gone."

The old man looked around, surprised. "Sam? He was here. Maybe he went with that man."

"What man?" My voice was sharp, harsh.

The old man shrank as if I'd hit him, trembled. "Some man. At the desk. Maybe Sam took him to his room."

"Where's Sam's room?"

He blinked. "Room?"

"Sam Shurk's room! Where is it?"

The old man began to cry again. "Back there. I don't know. Behind the desk. Somewhere."

I went through the door into the maze of silent rooms and corridors behind the registration desk. The doors of the dark rooms were all locked. Up and down the narrow side corridors I tried the doors. The light came from under the last door at the end of the side corridor nearest the back exit out into the alley. I pushed it open. A small room with a single light, narrow bed, bureau, bedside table and two armchairs. A worn rug on the floor.

Sam Shurk lay on the bed, one arm dangling, his head at an angle no living person's head could be, the red finger welts on his throat already turning purple. I bent over him. A thin trickle of blood oozed from his mouth. His neck had been broken. Snapped like a chicken's neck by powerful hands.

The telephone receiver hung from the bed table, swinging gently and buzzing with the dial tone.

I went out to the lobby and called the police from the registration desk.

Detective Lew Karnes wasn't any happier to see me this time than the last. He shoved me into a corner while his men went over the small room and spread out through the hotel. Maybe it was time to call Sid Bender after all, turn the lawyers loose on Karnes and his incompetent high hand.

"Give it to me," he said after I'd cooled long enough.

"I came to talk to Shurk. He was dead."

"That's it?"

To hell with him. Even I can get damned mad. This one I'd throw in his face when it was over.

"That's it."

"You're lying, Shaw."

"Arrest me. I'll take my call to Sid Bender, we'll see how the lawyers handle it."

He chewed on that, nose to nose. "Okay, you don't like me. I don't like P.I.'s. They work for themselves, hold out. Nothing personal, but you're doing it. How does this killing fit in with Luis Marquez?"

"I don't know that it does," I said. He got nothing.

"It has to." He looked at the dead clerk. "A big man. Big hands. Powerful. Why kill the clerk? No coincidence. This Luis Marquez turned out to be the owner of some bars up in East Harlem. Bars and some apartments. Maybe mixed up in gambling and smuggling illegal aliens. We're still checking him out. Probably into drugs, too, those spicks up there all are. So far no connection to anyone else you talked about."

It was his way of backing off. A kind of apology.

"There was that man in the Garous' room the night Marquez was shot," I said. "Maybe he came back and killed Shurk."

"Maybe," Karnes said. "Now all we got to do is find the Garous. Any ideas?"

"No," I said. "Can I go?"

"Shit then! Go on!"

I went. Out the back way and through the alley to Clinton Street. I didn't like Karnes and I had liked Sam Shurk. My eager helper. A nice little man who'd never had much in life or much chance to get much. Now he had no life. Why and who? I couldn't be sure it had been the man from Brooklyn. Anyone could have come in, back way or front way, while I was up in room 27. Anyone who had some motive to kill a nobody desk clerk in a cheap skid-row hotel. What motive? I didn't know, and I wasn't going to get any answers tonight. I wasn't going to get a taxi at this hour in the Bowery, either.

I walked the dark streets toward the places where there would be more lights and people, watched by unseen eyes that would roll me for my socks but that somehow knew better. As if they could sense the gun under my coat. Humans develop the senses needed to survive in whatever world they exist in. Sam Shurk had lost some of his survival senses, or he had moved, unaware, into a different world.

I reached Second Avenue and Houston Street before I found a cruising cab to pick me up. I was tired, but I hadn't got my messages at the office earlier before Sarah Jurgens had grabbed me. So before I went back to the Drake Hotel and Sarah, I stopped at the office. No one lurked in our antiseptic corridor. It was as bright and empty as an eternal corridor on some planet where life had died long ago, leaving only the machines operating on and on. Inside I switched on my solitary desk lamp, started the telephone answering machine and sat looking out over the late-night city as I listened to my calls.

Thayer was still in the hospital, he hoped I wasn't letting the office routine go to ruin. I was, our Finns took advantage of me all over the place when Thayer was out, and he knew it.

Maureen's agent wanted me to give her two messages, the studio wouldn't let him talk to her when she was on location.

A congressman I knew vaguely needed to talk to me professionally. He sounded nervous.

"Mr. Shaw?"

I sat up straight.

"Mr. Shaw, this is Sam Shurk. I've got something!"

I shut the machine off. For once I wished Thayer, Shaw and Delaney wasn't so damned modern. I could have used a bottle of Scotch in the bottom drawer. I turned the machine back on.

"This man just came around asking about a pawn ticket in room 27! He wanted to know if the cleaning woman had found one. He asked if anyone had found and turned in a pawn ticket anywhere in the hotel."

So that was what the man in the Datsun was looking for, or one thing. The pawn ticket I'd found in Matt Jurgens's study for the diamond bracelet Ted Garou had pawned. That was why I had been searched up in that East Harlem room. It tied the man to Ted Garou and his mother as I had guessed, and it tied the Garou pair to the Melville house and fund out in Brooklyn.

"I told him no one found a pawn ticket as far as I knew, but I hadn't talked to everyone. I said if he'd gimme his name and leave his address or phone number I could. . . ."

I leaned forward. I wanted to shout at that machine, "No, Sam, don't try to play detective! Don't try to find out about this man!" I wanted to warn him. *". . . He didn't want to leave his name, Mr. Shaw. Said he'd be back, I should hold anything for him, and you know, I think maybe I did see him before. Around the hotel, I mean. Not talkin' or askin' questions, just sort of 'around,' you know? Only a day or so ago. I'll bet he was the guy up there in that room . . . ahhhhhrrrrrrrr. . . ."*

A cry. One, that was all. Then the gasping for breath, the gagging, the horrible choking. The struggle of the dead man against the death that held his throat. A little man in a cheap hotel far across the city. The snap of his neck, and the silence. I closed my eyes, saw his body hanging limp in the thick hands of the killer. Then the dial tone began.

In the bathroom I couldn't throw up.

I sat. I held my head in my hands.

Because of me. A harmless little man, and I had killed him. Dead because he had tried to report to me. Loyal and eager. My "assistant." The man heard him and killed him. All because I had given a hotel clerk a few dollars. Because it had made him feel that he was doing something. Made him feel important. The poor, stupid little bastard.

I locked up and went down. I walked uptown to the Drake, breathing slow, deep. For the air. Because I was alive. To know that I was alive. At the Drake I didn't go up to Sarah Jurgens. Not tonight. I got my Ferrari and drove home. I went to bed. I didn't sleep well.

I lay staring up at the ceiling of my penthouse high above the city. Angry. I wanted this killer. I lay listening to the distant city far below. Angry at the cold-blooded killer and a little scared. After he had killed the helpless little clerk with his bare hands, he hadn't even bothered to hang up the telephone, just pressed down the cradle arm and walked out. A man who enjoyed killing. Out there somewhere now. And he knew more about me than I knew about him.

Fourteen

THE COOK WAS surly with my wake-up orange juice—I hadn't come home for either lunch or dinner. I fired her. I was in no mood to put up with someone else's temperament. I called the Drake while I dressed. Sarah Jurgens was still there but was taking no calls. To hell with her. In the kitchen the cook was crying. I rehired her, had coffee, toast and bacon, and went down to my Ferrari.

It was a cold, clear October morning with hard silver sunlight reflecting from the high windows of the city. I drove through the Battery Tunnel straight out to Brooklyn and around the steel blue winter Narrows past the towering Verrazano to Sheepshead Bay. The Melville semidetached was as silent as the quiet side street, no cars parked in the driveway or in front. I checked it out cautiously, but either it was unoccupied or everyone was asleep. If they were asleep, I wasn't going to wake them up. Not yet. I needed some more ammunition.

There was a lot more action around the storefront headquarters of the South Brooklyn Association on Emmons Avenue this time. I parked two blocks away on Ocean Avenue and walked back on the bay side of the street past all the piers of sport-fishing boats. Television trucks, police cars, radio cars, a fire truck and fifty other assorted vehicles packed the lot next to the association headquarters and the street in front, and a crowd of people spilled out of the store onto the sidewalk. I didn't see the blue Datsun among the cars or the silent man from last night among the people.

My blackmailing doll of a grandmother stood beaming at the front of the store as I pushed through as if I had some official purpose. She was happily looking toward the rear of the store where some cops, firemen and official-looking civilians kept the mob away from an open door into a back room. Through the doorway I could see bright, hot TV lights and the tail end of a hand-held video camera.

"Melvilles being interviewed?" I said.

Everyone's image of a grandmother looked at me and almost blushed. "Oh, hello. Did you, er, talk to them yourself?"

At least she remembered me and the tickets, and had the grace to be embarrassed.

"A fine family," I lied. "How's the picnic going?"

"Beautifully! So many people have been so very generous. The bike-a-thon is oversubscribed, and all the picnic tickets are sold! Now the TV people are filming the whole story of the fund, and it's going to be a special on the news at six tonight and tomorrow on the morning show."

"That should really start the bucks rolling in," I said. "I'll bet the Melvilles are excited. What did you say Mr. Melville's name was?"

"James," the old lady said. "And they're such modest people they act almost unhappy about how big the fund is growing as if they really don't want all the notice. The TV and all that."

"Modest," I said. "Tell me some more about them?

Where did you say they're from? What does Mr. Melville do?''

She frowned. ''I'm not sure where they're from. The South somewhere, I think. I think I told you that Mr. Melville was a construction worker, but he's had no work since they arrived in Brooklyn. He hasn't been well himself. He's done his best, odd jobs here and there, but it's been very hard for him to even keep the family fed, even with welfare. He could do nothing for the child. That's when Joel Young from our community weekly bulletin wrote the first story. He—''

''How did this Young hear about the Melvilles?''

''I think Mr. Melville came to the bulletin's office to ask about work opportunities, and they talked, and the poor child's illness came out.''

''Lucky,'' I said.

''Anyway, a local radio station picked up the story, and so did a large weekly newspaper here in Brooklyn. They came to us to offer their help. Even the police and the fire department, and our local American Legion and Chamber of Commerce, and our city councilman offered help. Everyone joined in the effort, and we got the fund started. We've had to use it for a wheelchair, special drugs and food, their rent, clothes, everything they need, but the main thrust is to have enough for the operation.''

''What operation?''

''Well, I don't understand it all myself, but it's some kind of bone-marrow operation and very expensive. Only a few medical centers can do it. But with this city-wide television exposure we should be able to raise more than enough.''

''But the Melvilles really hate all the fuss,'' I said.

''Isn't that the truth! Why, they're so shy they never even let anyone take their pictures. You'd never think that

Mr. Melville was so shy to look at him, but I can tell you the whole fund idea has been just agony for him. He's often said he thinks maybe they should just go home and all be together as long as they can. He hates charity so much. But Mrs. Melville says they have to give the child every chance so he has to agree.''

"Yeah," I said. "What's going to happen to the money? I mean, who actually gets it? Some hospital? A doctor? The Melvilles themselves?''

"Oh, I suppose we'll present Mr. Melville with the check, perhaps at the picnic.''

I looked around at the crowd so eager to see and to be seen. The fine, kind, charitable people only trying to help a sick child. Those who had thought of the fund in the first place, wanting only to help people so unfortunate, a child in pain, a family struck by tragedy in a cold world. All pressing forward, staring into the back room of the association's headquarters, watching the TV cameras, hoping to be noticed, pointed out as heroes. What I couldn't see from the door was the Melvilles. I could hear them, the nervous voice of a woman inside the back room, the soft voice of a boy underneath the bright public voice of the TV interviewer. I couldn't see them, but I had a strong feeling I knew who they were, and what was really going on.

"Any chance of getting around this crowd?" I asked my busy grandmother.

"There's a back door, but we always keep it locked.''

"Well, I think I'll get some air.''

I pushed back through the edge of the crowd into the cool morning of Emmons Avenue. The parking lot was to my left. I slipped through it, looking for the back door, keeping my eyes open for the battered Datsun. There was no sign of the small blue car. That could mean my theory about the Melvilles was wrong, but I didn't think so. The rear door was on a narrow alley that ran behind the Emmons Avenue shops. As my larcenous grandmother had said, the door was locked. There was no one behind the buildings to see me use my tools on the lock, and I was bent to the lock when I heard a click and jumped back just in time to keep from being knocked flat on my back. The man who came out looked back into the room. I made it to cover behind the nearest car.

Assorted rubberneckers came out first, followed by the TV camera crew walking backward with their equipment and aiming the camera back into the headquarters room, and then the interviewer surrounded by the smiling politicians and local philanthropists. Then I saw the Melvilles. And the Garous.

The boy sat looking stoical and brave in a wheelchair, small, thin, pale, with those large luminous eyes that watched everyone from a distance. Eyes that still hadn't found whatever he looked for, a faint curl to his thin lips that could be pain or contempt.

Only a few inches taller than the boy, with her well-curved figure and pretty face, the mother pushed the wheelchair through the crowd. Pale, her good color gone, she looked every year of the thirty-eight I had guessed at the Grace Hotel.

The man walked beside the wheelchair, his hand heavy on the boy's shoulder, smiling humbly at the interviewer and the camera. The thick, silent driver of the battered blue Datsun with the soft, inexorable walk. In his shabby brown suit again, the smile thin and stiff as if he hardly knew how to smile, as humble as he could ever get.

Melville and Garou. One and the same. The unemployed man who crushed beer cans and watched TV alone, the go-go dancer who still carried her publicity photos with her and the boy who had walked through the lobby of the Grace Hotel as normally as anyone.

When the final ceremony was over, to the last shots of the TV camera, Ted Garou/Melville and the mother got into a gray Chevy with Louisiana plates as battered as the blue Datsun. "James Melville" climbed into a black limousine with the city councilman and the television interviewer, and the limo headed off behind the TV truck toward the nearest parkway entrance. The gray Chevy and most of the other cars headed in the opposite direction.

I followed the Chevy and the parade. They led me to the semidetached on the quiet side street and, as everyone trooped into the house behind the boy in the wheelchair, I continued on past and parked up the street again. Smoking, I watched. The parade of well-wishers, gawkers, freeloaders, whatever and whoever they were, began to leave almost at once as if they had only escorted the "Melvilles" home as a kind of honor guard. They came out in small groups and drove off until the street was empty and quiet once more. I moved fast. The man might show up again anytime, but for the moment I had them alone.

The curtains moved at a living-room window when I rang. No one came to the door. I continued to ring. Eventually it was the woman who opened the door. She stood on the glassed-in porch, frowning at me, small and uneasy, but somehow with the fluid grace of a dancer.

"Yes?"

"Mrs. Melville? I represent the Sanston Medical Foundation of San Vicente, California. May I come in?"

She paled. "Come in?"

"To talk to you? Perhaps you've heard of the Sanston Foundation? We sponsor research in catastrophic diseases, especially in children, and make rather large grants. Your son's case has come to our attention, we are considering a grant but must have some specific information.''

"I don't know. Mr. . . . Melville handles all that.''

I wanted to say, "I'll bet he does," but instead I looked at my watch, did my frown and went into my pressure act. "I really must have the basic details to send to my committee today, or we may not be able to move on this in time. Our usual contribution covers the entire cost of the full course of treatment and would be entirely separate from the community fund your kind neighbors have so generously established, but we must move.''

She licked at her full lips, even more uneasy now that I had indicated that a lot of money was involved. As if it wasn't the money she wanted but something else. Or as if it wasn't *she* who wanted the money, and she was afraid either to accept it or to turn it down, afraid to make a mistake. But I had her uncertain, hesitating, and took the advantage. As I talked, I slowly moved her back across the porch and into the living room.

"What I need now, Mrs. Melville, is the background of the boy and his illness. Place of birth, date of birth, when you first discovered his illness, the names of the doctors—''

She grew paler and shook her head, "Like I told you, mister, Ja—his father got to tell you about all those things. I—''

By now we were in the living room, and I saw the boy across the room in his wheelchair, watching television as if he hardly knew I was there. But he knew, and I changed my show now that I was in and alone with them.

"All right, Mrs. Garou, you can drop the act. Ted can get up from that wheelchair and walk around the way he was before I rang the bell. What did you want from Matt Jurgens?''

For a long couple of seconds of silence I thought she was going to fall right down on the floor of the living room. She held onto the edge of the television set.

"You're . . . you're not from any foundation."

Ted Garou turned his wheelchair toward me. "Ma?"

"Who are you anyway?" I had lied to her.

"What does he want, ma?" Ted Garou said. "Who is he?"

"I don't know," she said, stared at me. "Cop?"

"Just someone who followed a pawn ticket to the Grace Hotel and knows a con game when he sees one. A sweet little sting on the good, dumb people of South Brooklyn."

"It wasn't our idea!" the boy cried. "That's why we ran out, went to the Grace! This was all Jack's idea!"

"The man in the blue Datsun?"

The woman nodded. "He came after us. Told them we'd gone off for treatment, tracked us down and found us. Two weeks, but he found us."

"Jack who?"

"Jack Garou." Her voice was shaky, bitter. "My husband. Virginia, Ted and Jack Garou, that's us. A swell team."

"Where does Matt Jurgens fit into the picture?"

"He doesn't!" Ted Garou said. "You said you wasn't no cop! Ma, he's a cop, don't say no more."

Virginia Garou suddenly sat down on the couch. "What difference does it make? He knows about the con game anyway."

"I'm a private detective, that's all," I said. "I'm working for Sarah Jurgens, I don't care about the swindle. I want to know what you wanted from Matt Jurgens, what you were doing at his house, and what happened the night he was murdered."

"We don't know nothin' about the night Jurgens got

killed,'' Ted Garou said. He was standing now. He wore small canvas running shoes.

"You always wear shoes like that?" I asked.

"I wear all kinds of shoes!"

"Maybe, but you were there the night Matt Jurgens—"

I stopped because Virginia Garou stood up as suddenly as she had sat down. She stared at me, but she wasn't seeing me. She was listening. To a car that seemed to slow down as it passed by on the quiet street. Before the car passed on, while it seemed about to stop, the expression on her face was sheer terror. I looked at Ted Garou. The boy held to the arm of his wheelchair, as pale as a corpse. It was he who finally spoke, his voice raw and strained.

"You got to get out of here, mister. You'll get us all killed!"

Virginia Garou nodded violently. "Please! He could come back any minute. He'll find you here!"

"Let him," I snapped. "I want to talk to him, too."

"You're crazy, mister," Ted Garou said.

"No, please, you don't understand," Virginia Garou cried, "Jack—"

"What was your connection to Matt Jurgens?" I said.

Virginia Garou literally wrung her hands, pleaded with me, "Jack's a terrible man, Mr. Shaw! He's a violent man. A gangster! He's dangerous."

"A bank robber!" the boy said. "He's killed people!"

I remembered what Freddie the Writer, my skid-row stoolie, had said: "They're scared in the alleys. The kid scares them. They know he's rolling the alleys, but they don't want any part of stopping him, catching him. Something about him, some connection, scares them. . . ." It was Jack Garou who had scared them in the alleys. Garou searching around skid row for the boy and his mother, maybe for the whole two weeks. That was why no one wanted any part of Ted Garou no matter whom he robbed. They had heard about who his father was, and no one wanted any trouble with Jack Garou in the dark world of skid row. A killer and a gangster. I believed them. I'd seen Jack Garou up close.

"Did Garou kill Matt Jurgens?"

Virginia Garou shook her head. "I don't know. Why would he? Please, he's terrible, he's got guns, I'm afraid—"

"Did Ted there spot the money and tell Garou? Is that what happened? Garou went to the house and killed Jurgens for the money?"

"Money?" Virginia Garou said.

"What money?" Ted Garou said. "He didn't tell me about no money."

"Fifty thousand," I said. "In the house."

"Oh, God," Virginia Garou said.

Ted sat down. "Jack must of followed me."

"The poor man," Virginia Garou said.

"You think Garou did murder Jurgens for the money?"

"It was there, wasn't it?" Ted Garou said. "All he had to do was tail me from the Grace. Maybe he found us there earlier, watched us."

"Maybe," I said. "Only what were you doing with Matt Jurgens in the first place?"

"Why shouldn't I of been with Jurgens?" Ted Garou said, angry. "He—"

Virginia Garou heard it first, turned toward the kitchen doorway. The boy began to shake where he stood up again and held to the arm of his wheelchair. A quick, light footstep. And another. I heard, and I knew the soft step of Jack Garou. I reached for my gun. Too late.

"No way," the cold voice said. "Too bad, mister."

He stood in the doorway with the .357 Magnum I'd last seen in the Datsun aimed at me. He looked at Ted Garou where he stood beside the wheelchair, then back at me, and his eyes told me that I'd seen what I shouldn't have seen. Virginia Garou saw his eyes. She stepped toward him between us. Jack Garou watched his wife, his face impassive. Then his head moved. Perhaps an inch.

"Out of the way, Ginny."

"Jack, no!"

"Shit! Out of my way!"

That odd quickness for such a thick, squat man brought him to his wife in a step. She grabbed at his gun arm.

"Run!" she cried. "Run!"

I ran. For the doorway to the glassed-in porch. Tried to get my gun from my shoulder harness. Garou knocked the woman to the floor, skirt and legs flying askew. I needed another five feet. The boy gave them to me, pushed his wheelchair into Garou's legs, knocking him off balance as he shot. The bullet smashed a window in the porch, and I hit the front door going hard. Then I was down the steps and running for the next driveway and the corner of the semidetached and around into cover.

And didn't stop there. Not even to get my gun out. Those few seconds, turning back, could be my last.

Ran on down the driveway, across the backyard to the fence, over it on my face and hands, and behind me Garou was shooting.

Over the fence, wood splinters ripping, and someone was beside me, above me where I sprawled, kneeling and firing a shot back toward where I had run from, shouting, "Garou! Right there! Hold it right. . . . Shit!"

Ducked beside me. Three shots splintered wood. I was up now, my gun out at last. There was no one to shoot at. Not in the yard or the driveway. My rescuer swore.

"God damn it!"

He was a tall, thin man as he stood up. Rawboned and

stoop-shouldered. Angry. I knew him. The second man who had found me tied to the chair up in that silent East Harlem room. A man who had rescued me twice now.

"That's two I owe you," I said. "Mr. . . . ?"

He glared over the fence at the empty driveway, chewed on his lip, ignored me.

"He's got a goddamned shooting gallery," he raged.

There was no cover at all between the fence and the houses.

"The garage over there's closer to his half, but there's still a lot of open space to cross," I said.

"Damn you, Shaw! You blew it for me! Too damned soon. Another day or two and I'd have had him with the cash in his pocket. All damned P.I.'s should be jailed!"

We both heard the car start, the screech of tires as it drove away, saw the flash of blue as it passed on the street.

"Hell!"

He climbed the fence, and we walked up the driveway toward the front, warily but rapidly now. The front door into the glassed-in porch was open, and inside Virginia Garou sat on the floor of the living room, her face held in her hands. The boy, Ted, lay beside the broken wheelchair. There was blood on his face. As we came in, he crawled across the floor to his mother, knelt beside her.

"Ma? It's okay. He's gone, ma."

She nodded but didn't look up. The boy touched her with his skinny hand.

"Ma? Ma, maybe this time—"

She looked up now. "He always comes back." She was a mess. Her left eye was swollen shut, the bruise around it spreading purple and yellow already. There was blood on her lower lip. It would be puffed like a balloon. A bruise on her left cheekbone. All from more than the one blow. Jack Garou had taken the time to give them both a lesson about getting in his way before he ran, a warning and perhaps a promise. "I'm sorry, Ted. He always finds me. He always comes back. He always will. I know that."

Ted wiped the blood from his scrawny face.

"It's okay, ma. Someday—"

The depth of the hate in the boy's eyes was bottomless. I didn't want to be Jack Garou when he was old and the boy was a man. But that was me. Garou would laugh at the boy even as he died.

"Someday," my double rescuer said, "he'll sit in the chair, and you'll sit on his lap. Where'd he go, Virginia?"

Virginia Garou wiped blood from her lip. "Do I know you?"

"Cop, ma," Ted said. "That's why Jack ran."

"Lucky for you two," my man said. "Lieutenant Rothberg, Manhattan Central Bunco. The scam's over. Where'd Garou go?"

Virginia Garou said, "You think he'd tell us after doing this to us?"

"Don't con me, girl. You three been working as a team a long time. You know where he went. Where to meet him."

"He don't tell no one where he goes when he's runnin'," Ted Garou said. "He just goes, comes back anytime he wants."

"Hell!" Rothberg swore. "I guess I got to take just you two in. Shaw, you really screwed me good, damn it. Made me move too soon and too open. I oughta kick your—"

The voice came, metallic, loud and distorted. From somewhere outside. "YOU IN THERE! LAY DOWN YOUR WEAPONS! YOU'RE SURROUNDED AND UNDER DIRECT OBSERVATION. THIS IS THE POLICE. LAY DOWN YOUR—"

Through the living-room window I saw a cop at the window of the next house, riot gun aimed. At the back door beyond the kitchen there was a flash of blue.

"The shooting," I said. "Someone called."

"Jesus Christ!" Lieutenant Rothberg raged, strode out into the porch. "Knock it off, you jerks! This is Rothberg, Manhattan Central Bunco, making a goddamn arrest!"

There was numb silence. I listened but heard no one move on the street. Rothberg was almost jumping up and down in frustration. He was having a bad day.

He shouted. "What do you clowns out there think you've got, an invasion? Look!" He came back into the living room and pushed us out onto the glassed-in porch. "Here, two boosters—a kid and a broad, one two-bit private eye and a Bunco lieutenant! Maybe you should send for a S.W.A.T. team!"

There was another silence on the street and around the semidetached. I felt my neck crawl. We were in a glass fishbowl. The voice that finally spoke through the bullhorn was cold and not amused.

"OKAY, MISTER, IF YOU'RE WHAT YOU SAY YOU ARE, YOU KNOW HOW TO COME OUT. HANDS UP, WALK SLOW."

We went out, hands high in the air. Except Rothberg. That far he wasn't going with precinct clowns, that would be too much. But I noticed that his hands were in clear sight so that they could be seen to be empty. He wasn't a fool.

A uniformed captain came to meet us.

The Bunco detective showed his shield.

"We got a report of shooting," the captain said. "I take shooting mighty seriously. What's your story?"

"I've been on this damned con for a month and after Jack Garou for a long time. I've been tailing Garou all over town, wanted to wait until the big loot was in his hands before I grabbed him. But Shaw here, the goddamn private eye, just blew the whole damn thing.''

"Jack Garou?'' The captain was staring at Ted Garou standing as well as anyone. "What's he got to do with the Melvilles?''

Rothberg laughed. "He *is* the Melvilles. The three of them used the name before in their scams.''

The captain's face got red. "You're sure about that?''

"Hell, Jack Garou's got a record as long as both our arms in half the country. Con games, muggings, holdups, robberies, you name it.''

The captain's face got redder. "We better go down to the station and check this all out.''

"I got to take my prisoners in,'' Rothberg protested.

"Mister,'' the captain said, "right now you don't have no prisoners, we do. You don't have this Jack Garou at all. We go to the station house.''

Rothberg swore, but there was nothing he could do. The cops herded us into squad cars and drove us to their station house. The captain didn't get any happier on the ride, and neither did his men. I didn't need E.S.P. to know what the problem was. They had helped the Melville Fund, promoted the cause of the poor little boy dying of leukemia in his wheelchair. They had been "had'' along with all the other suckers, and they were going to give Rothberg and me a hard time. We had known about the Garous and hadn't told them. Now we knew they'd been conned, could tell the world, and they were in no hurry to let us go on our way. Especially Rothberg. He was a fellow cop.

It took them a couple of hours, but they finally checked me out by calling my office, Thayer in the hospital, Lieutenant Guevara out in Douglaston and Lew Karnes at Manhattan East.

"Okay, Shaw. Karnes says you're a pain in the ass who don't cooperate with the police, but you can go," the captain said. "Only next time you come into my precinct, you come to me first."

Rothberg was still cooling his heels and cursing them all when I left the squad room. It was going to be a very long morning for him.

Fifteen

THERE WAS A pay phone in the dingy second-floor corridor of the station house. I called the Drake Hotel in Manhattan. Sarah Jurgens had checked out early this morning leaving a message for me: "Gone home. Come."

I retrieved my car keys and car from the police, and took the Belt Parkway around the city past the salt marshes of Jamaica Bay, where clumps of tract houses seemed to have grown straight up out of the mud and bulrushes, to Little Neck Bay with its own mud flats and rushes. On Northern Boulevard I crawled with the noon traffic to Douglaston. The first thing I noticed was that the police car was gone from the driveway of the Jurgens house.

"Come in, Paul!"

She wore slacks now. Gray slacks and a dark blue sweater, subdued, with her hair tied back at the nape of her neck and little makeup. She raised on her toes to kiss me, clung a moment.

"I waited." She almost pouted. "You should have come back to the hotel."

"It got too late," I said.

Her voice was coy. "You're going to resist yourself right out of something really good, Mr. Shaw." And then she

changed abruptly. Serious and composed, and yet with an
eagerness. "I told Lieutenant Guevara about the fifty
thousand dollars Matt took from the office. He was very
excited, said they had been getting nowhere because they
couldn't really find a motive. The possibility of fifty thousand dollars being in the house changed everything. It gave
them something to dig for—some thief or transient spend-
ing a lot of money! Perhaps anyone who knew Matt and
seemed to suddenly have extra money. The lieutenant says
he's sure now that it was some burglar or transient who
somehow saw Matt with the money and tried to grab it."

"Maybe," I said and then told her what had happened
since I'd left her at the Drake last night. From the man
following her being Peter Jellicoe, to Jack Garou, the murder of Sam Shurk and the "Melville" sting out in Brooklyn.

She listened with a face of growing confusion. "What
do most of those people have to do with Matt? Or with
his murder? What are Estelle and Peter *doing?* Why was
that Garou boy here with Matt? Did the boy know about
the fifty thousand dollars? Is that why Matt had the money?
It was some kind of blackmail after all, Paul? Or did that
gangster kill poor Matt for the money? Or those Latin
people, whoever they are? Maybe they're rival gangs! That
Carmen in Matt's office, she might have known about the
fifty thousand dollars. Maybe those Latins killed him!"

"They're all possibles," I agreed, "but somehow I
think the boy is still the key. Was Matt in New Orleans
in, say, 1966? Did he ever mention the name Garou? Or
maybe a go-go dancer named Virginia?"

She shook her head slowly, "He's been in New Orleans
many times, of course. He has . . . had at least one client
company down there, perhaps more, I'm not sure. He al-

ways liked that jazz they play down there, I never could understand why. I hate all that kind of music. He—''

I stopped her with a raised finger, held up my open hand for silence. I had heard the faint noise. Something against the side of the house. A light contact noise as if a hand or a knee had inadvertently touched the wood a little harder than it should have. Someone was outside close to the windows.

Leaving Sarah apparently still talking to me in an unseen corner, I slipped through the kitchen, out the back door and around the house. He was crouched directly under the living-room window where someone had watched the night of the murder. Peter Jellicoe.

''You going to try to run,'' I said, ''or come inside?''

He jumped up as if bitten. For a moment I thought he was going to try to fight. He was a lot bigger and younger than I was. I had my hand on my gun.

''Talking is easier,'' I said. ''You'll have to talk to us sooner or later.''

He collapsed, almost literally. Seemed to grow physically smaller as he walked ahead of me into the house.

Sarah Jurgens lighted a cigarette, said low and almost vicious, ''Spying on me? Following me? What do you think you're doing? Tell me. Under *my* window.''

Peter Jellicoe shrugged. ''Seeing what you were up to.''

''Up to?'' The cigarette poised, astonished and furious. ''Up to! You punk! You . . . juvenile idiot! I'll fire you, so help me! She put you up to it, didn't she? Estelle! Well, she just got you fired! Go tell my sweet sister-in-law that!''

''Easy,'' I said. I put my hand on her shoulder to calm her. Her muscles were rigid under her skin, tense and almost quivering. There was a rage in her, but I felt the tight muscles relax under my touch. "Let's hear what he has to say."

She breathed hard and deeply, and sat down. Slowly she began to smoke the cigarette again, to blow the smoke in a long stream into the silence of the room, all without ever moving her eyes from Peter Jellicoe's face. Cold, angry eyes.

"Okay," I said to Jellicoe, "you were under the window. I think you've been listening under that window before. I—"

"That's a lie!" Jellicoe turned on me.

"Maybe," I said, "but you've been tailing Sarah, and you've been snooping around El Jazz Latino and the Grace Hotel. Why?"

"Because I damn well felt like it," Jellicoe said. As if this small show of macho resistance made him feel better, he sat down on the living-room couch and firmly raised his jaw.

"You're awfully close to looking for a job," Sarah Jurgens said.

I watched the determination fade from the pale, sullen eyes and the handsome face that was bland and restless at the same time. He looked for a moment, all six feet four and two hundred and ten pounds, like some boy whose parents have gone off to Europe leaving him alone on the empty campus of a boarding school at Christmas. Then he suddenly shrugged.

"Go ahead and fire me. I never wanted the job much anyway, not really."

I heard a different note in his voice, a sudden feeling of reality and something almost like relief.

"What did you want?" I asked.

"I don't know," he said.

"If you don't care about the agency, why are you snooping around?"

He thought about that. "For Estelle, I suppose."

"You always do what your mother asks?"

"I guess so." He shrugged again. "My father walked out on us."

"Why did your mother want you to nose around?"

He didn't really want to tell me, had made up his mind that he wouldn't tell me. But he had the kind of soft easy-going mind that would eventually tell you almost anything if you asked long enough, surrounded him with questions from different angles. And he didn't want to be fired, not really.

He shrugged a third time nervously. "She's sure Matt was up to something outside the office that wasn't company business, and maybe that's what got him killed. We've been trying to find out what and who and all that. I mean, who are all these crazy people showing up? So I've been watching and trying to figure some of it out."

"What did you find out so far?"

"Nothing," Jellicoe said. "Absolutely nothing at all. Zero. I lost everyone and never even saw anyone tailing me! Got caught cold under the window. Not my kind of work, is it? I'm no good at it. I'm no good at anything except maybe working with my hands. Woodworking. Cabinetmaking. I can do that, you know?"

"What about running Jurgens Associates?"

"I don't know, maybe I could. I guess I could. That's what Estelle wants. Got to be an executive. Her son."

Sarah Jurgens smoked another cigarette. "That'll be the day. If you're lucky, maybe I'll let you handle some accounts."

"So fire me and get it over with!"

"Maybe I'll just do that!"

"So do it!"

They were shouting in the quiet room. Straight at each other. It didn't sound to me as if either of them wanted to follow through, just a family steam letting.

"Woodworking," I said in a lull as they glared at each other, "is that what you want to do, Jellicoe?"

"Money and the easy life! That's what he wants," Sarah said, fury still in her voice. "Him and his snotty mother. Maybe fifty thousand dollars? A nice start, right, Junior?"

"Me?" Jellicoe was up on his feet. They had been shouting at each other from their seats, but now Jellicoe stood. "You took that money! Don't try to hide behind me! I—"

"Liar!"

She was on him before I could move. He pushed her off, and I grabbed her, but not before she'd left three long streaks of blood on his cheek. He used his handkerchief on his face, his pale eyes horrified at the sight of his own blood, his hand shaky as if in great pain from the "wounds." I felt her whole body as hard as stone as she strained toward him.

"You're after that money. . . . or maybe you already have it! You and your bitch of a mother! Accusing me! How would you know even if I did have it, eh? You couldn't know, you stupid liar! Just another of your stupid attempts to hurt me and grab my agency!"

Jellicoe went on dabbing at the long livid scratches on his face. The marks had begun to swell into welts. Jellicoe's eyes winced as he dabbed gently, blinking toward Sarah. Pain is relative, and you need experience to handle anything.

"What makes you think Sarah has the fifty thousand?" I asked.

He held the handkerchief to his face. "Who else would have it? No one's found the money, have they?"

"That's it?" I said. "A guess? A hunch?"

"She made me damned mad." He looked at the blood on his handkerchief, then up at Sarah Jurgens. "Firing me like that. No one likes to be fired."

"We'll talk at the office," Sarah said.

I had the sense of missing something. A rapport between them, a communication. Maybe only that in the end it was always best to keep the money and power in the family.

"What did you see when you were snooping around," I said. "At El Jazz Latino? At the Grace Hotel? Anywhere?"

"Not a damned thing. I told you. I guess I don't even know what to look for." He sighed, down on himself.

Unless he was leading me up the path, knew exactly what he had been looking for and had perhaps found it.

"Does the name Jack Garou mean anything to you?" I described Garou to him. "Seen him anywhere around?"

"I'm not sure." He frowned. "Maybe. Somewhere around."

"At Penn Station?"

He shook his head slowly. "No, earlier. Maybe at that jazz club. Around there anyway."

It wasn't much, but it was something. Jack Garou had had an El Jazz Latino matchbook in his battered Datsun, and unless he'd got it from Matt Jurgens, alive or dead, he must have been around the club at some time and might be again.

While I thought about it, Peter Jellicoe stood dabbing at his scratched face and watching both of us. Neither Sarah nor I said anything. After a time he turned toward the door. Slowly, as if he expected to be stopped, and then walked on faster and out, his back stiff all the way like someone waiting for a knife. Outside, his car started and faded.

"You still going to fire him?" I asked Sarah.

She lighted another cigarette. "I'll talk to Harry Glanz and the board in the office."

"You might need Junior after all."

"No sense making changes too soon."

"No," I said. "I'll be back."

She smiled. "You'd better."

Sixteen

St. Marks Place teemed as it did on any afternoon, weekday or weekend. Surging and thinning, a river of people. El Jazz Latino neither teemed nor surged. I had to park two blocks away, and the front door of the club was closed and locked. It had never been locked before and was due to open in only a few hours. There should have been light and activity inside.

There was some light but no activity. Faint light distant among the shadows through the single small pane of glass in the front door, but no movement anywhere. I walked around the block to the alley off Ninth Street and the side door of the club. It was open. I stumbled over the body just inside the door.

The middle-aged mop man.

I bent over him. There was too much blood to see what had killed him.

My gun was in my hand. I didn't have to see what had killed the mop man. Something that left a hole big enough for a lot of blood. Maybe a .357 Magnum. In the hands of a killer. Somewhere in the city. Or in the dim room?

The only light in the vast basement room with its looming pillars and shadowed tables came from the work light at the end of the long bar and another far back near the rest rooms. The drums were still on the bandstand waiting for the night. The club was neat, clean, ready to open and empty. So silent I could hear even the voices of people passing out in the light of the street.

I moved. Slowly. Listening. Through the shadows left and right toward the long bar. Waiting for a movement, a sound of someone else. There was nothing. Only the heavy silence, my gun probing ahead. To the bar, stools lying on their sides, broken glass, a pungent odor of spilled whiskey and a man on the floor behind the bar with an automatic.

"You take chances . . . *amigo.*"

The gray-haired owner with the long Spanish face lay propped up against the floor cabinets out of sight of the rest of the club, his dark eyes still steady, and the gun pointed at me. But there was rigid pain just under the surface of the Castilian face, his short, broad chest heaving slowly as he breathed very softly. His left hand held his side, and at each shallow breath a small spurt of blood came from between his fingers. His voice was low and slow, his small smile still amused by this world.

"How bad is it?" I asked.

"Not as wide as the ocean but . . . enough."

The faint smile, but the Cholo accent and act were gone. He had more important matters on his mind.

"I'll get a doctor," I said.

"Carmen already went for one. Shaw . . . listen—"

"Talk after the doctor's been," I said.

He shook his head. Blood spurted through the fingers pressed to his side. He waited, breathing slowly and quietly until the bleeding stopped and the pain passed. When he spoke again, it was even more slowly and carefully, timing the spasms of pain and blood to pause as little as possible.

"Listen, Shaw. I'll make it, but maybe . . . pass out. Listen, I didn't like you not saying Matt Jurgens was dead as if you were trying to trap me. Later we knew you worked for the . . . wife. Meme didn't like that. She—"

"Meme? Who is she?"

"The woman who talked to you . . . in Harlem. In the red Cutlass . . . was in here with us the other time." The blood trickled. He breathed, waited. "Listen, he came in here maybe an hour ago . . . crazy wild. Anglo. The man you asked about . . . I think."

"Jack Garou?" I described Garou.

He nodded, breathed hard. "He had a gun. He wanted to know who we were . . . why we were interested in Matt . . . Jurgens. He wanted to know why Luis Marquez was in that hotel . . . what was Luis doing coming after him? He asked us where the bracelet was? Did we have the pawn ticket? Where was the money?"

"What did you say?"

"That we didn't know what he was talking about. He went . . . crazy. He threatened us, said he'd killed Luis with his own gun, and he'd kill . . . us. Emiliano tried to jump him. . . ." He closed his eyes with the pain. For himself and for the dead mop man. "Carmen was in the back. The girl who worked for Matt Jurgens. She heard the shots that killed Emiliano and came out. I suppose he . . . thought she was some danger, he was awfully . . . jumpy even with the gun."

"The police are looking for him already," I said.

"I was afraid. . . ." He didn't finish, opened his eyes at me. "He grabbed Meme. I tried for the gun under the bar. He shot me and went out. The police are after him, and they don't know he's got Meme."

I heard the quick footsteps out in the alley. The door opened behind me. I turned fast. Carmen, the swarthy driver of the red Cutlass who didn't like my humorous attitude, one of the skinny little Latins who'd escorted me up in East Harlem and an older Latin in a dark suit and carrying a black bag came into the club. The mustachioed driver went for his gun.

"No!" The owner raised his voice. "It's okay, Rafael. He can help. We need help . . . now."

The driver settled back. He didn't like me any better, began his almost soundless whistling. The little silent man watched the door. Carmen and the older man with the black bag hurried to the fallen owner behind the bar. I talked while the doctor worked.

"You knew nothing about the Garous, the bracelet, the pawn ticket or the money Matt Jurgens had at home?"

"We knew about the money," the owner said. His gun lay on the floor now, his gun hand pressed to the floor, his other hand gripping a cabinet door as the doctor worked on his side.

"We don' know who got it," Carmen said. She watched me with hostility, no happier than the driver whistling his soundless Latin song.

The owner went pale as the doctor worked, his hand white on the cabinet door.

"Hospital, Estaban," the doctor said. "You're going to pass out."

"Wait, Doctor!" Estaban said. "Shaw, listen. He killed Luis, he probably . . . killed Matt Jurgens. He's got Meme, the cops want him. I can't do anything now. You've got to find him, get Meme—"

"Who is Meme, Estaban?" I said. "You haven't told me yet. Who was Luis? What is their connection to Matt Jurgens and the Garous?"

The driver stopped whistling. "Hey, Estaban! We don' need this Anglo peeper! Don' tell him nothin'!"

"We'll find Meme ourselves!" Carmen echoed.

"No," Estaban said. The doctor and the driver helped him shakily to his feet, his side bandaged, his hand gripping the bar. "We need him. He knows what's happening. He can work with . . . the police." He faced me. "Luis Marquez was a big man up in East Harlem. Clubs, bookies, card parlors, maybe drugs. This Garou said he knew all that . . . we'd have to pay to get Meme back." He breathed hard and shallow with the effort of talking. "But Luis wasn't working at his business when Garou killed him, he was just helping Meme find out who murdered Matt Jurgens. By now they're fighting to take over up in Harlem, they won't care who killed Luis or what happens to Meme."

"Why was Luis helping Meme?"

Carmen said, "Because she's Remedios Marquez, Luis's sister."

"What else was she?"

The owner, Estaban, said, "Matt Jurgens's girl friend."

"Not just girl friend," Carmen said. "A lot more his wife than the 'duchess' out in Douglaston. For a long time, too. His wife never knew what he was or gave a damn what he wanted. He knew they had nothin' a long time ago, but he didn't want to hurt her, you know? She always wanted kids but couldn't have any. She married him to have kids, he felt he owed her. Guilt, right? A lot of men are like that, especially Anglos."

Estaban said, "Matt Jurgens loved music, Shaw. Jazz, mariachi, flamenco. He played guitar, had been coming to this club for years, always sat in with any band we had. He played all kinds of guitar and pretty well. He played in clubs and with bands all over the country, anytime he went on a trip anywhere for his agency. For a lot longer than he came in here, I think.'' He leaned against the bar and held on, in pain and breathing irregularly. The doctor motioned to the driver. Estaban waved him away. ''I guess what he always wanted was to be a musician. Live like a musician, be with musicians. . . . But he had a wife to support, got started in public relations and advertising, and couldn't change.''

''Meme's a singer,'' Carmen said. ''They was good together. All the years Matt would never leave that wife. He said he'd never put her through no divorce. He didn't want the house, or the agency, or most of the money, or anything else he had. All he wanted was to get out, put it all behind him, break clean, an' that's what he was gonna do. He an' Meme was gonna break out at last, go down to Mexico, start a whole new life. She was all excited. She was happy. Then Matt was killed.''

''Why the sudden change? Going away together?''

Carmen shook her head. ''I don' know. Meme didn't know. She didn't care why.''

''Where do the Garous fit in all of it?''

They were silent, looked at each other. No one knew.

''Why was Luis Marquez at the Grace Hotel?''

The swarthy driver said, ''Meme saw the boy with Jurgens. We tailed the kid to that hotel, and Luis went up to talk to him.''

''What was the boy's connection to Matt Jurgens?''

''We don' know,'' Carmen said. ''That's what Luis was gonna find out.''

The driver said, ''We didn't even know there was a guy in the room.''

''He wasn't supposed to be there,'' I said.

Estaban said, ''Find him, Shaw. Get him. And get Meme back alive. We can pay you.''

"I'll do what I can," I said, "but it's a job for the cops. You go to them. And right now."

The driver, Rafael, moved back. "Hey, man!"

"The cops?" Carmen cried. "They'll get her killed!"

"No," Estaban said again. "He's right. We have to go to the police, tell them Garou is holding Meme hostage. They've got to know, and they have to know Garou's a killer."

I said, "Tell them everything, the whole story. And tell them fast."

"You?" Estaban said, watching me as he held to the bar.

I shrugged. "Try to find Jack Garou before the cops."

Seventeen

THE AFTERNOON HAD darkened, the sky to the east building to a storm again, a gray wind rising along the Narrows and Gravesend Bay. October almost November in the vast city where a cold killer ran with Meme Marquez as hostage, the heavy clouds and wind gripping me like some giant hand as I parked at the South Brooklyn precinct station where they were holding Virginia and Ted Garou. Or where they had held them.

"A hot lawyer and bail money," the desk sergeant told me. "We let 'em go twenty minutes ago. Bunco is screaming, but the lawyer got a judge to set fast bail."

"Who paid the lawyer, put up the cash?"

"The shyster's Saul Cromwell. Want his address? He set it all up, it's all I know."

"Maybe later," I said.

Logic said they would go back to their semidetached, at least for their car and possessions, so I drove under the coming storm to the quiet back street. The gray Chevy with Louisiana plates was parked in the driveway, and so was a low black Porsche convertible. I recognized the Porsche and knew who had hired the hotshot lawyer and put up the bail money. I went in without knocking. They were all in the living room: Virginia Garou on the couch again; Ted Garou near her on the floor; Peter Jellicoe at the side window, looking out at the dingy little yard as if he'd never seen anything that poor before; and Estelle Jellicoe in the middle of the room as if she'd been doing most of the talking.

"Nice," I said. "How long have you four been a team?"

"Team?" Virginia Garou said. "I don't understand, Mr. Shaw? We—"

"They get Jurgens Associates," I said, "and you split the fifty thousand. Nice deal."

"Hey," Ted Garou got up from the floor. "We don't know these people! They just showed up with a lawyer and bailed us out. I mean, they just helped us."

"They found out who you were and where you were and what was happening by E.S.P. ? Voices on the wind?"

Virginia Garou looked ready to cry. "I told you we should have said no, Ted. Nobody bails you out for nothin'."

"You told us who they were and where and what was happening, Mr. Shaw," Estelle Jellicoe said. "We never met them before this afternoon."

"I told you?"

"When you told Sarah this morning," Peter Jellicoe said from the window. He didn't turn, went on looking out as if waiting for something to appear. "I heard it all."

Estelle Jellicoe smiled. "Listening under windows has its rewards."

"So," Peter said, "we came to find out how they knew Matt."

"To find out what Matt was doing when he should have been working for the agency," Estelle Jellicoe said.

"Probably what got him murdered. We have a right to know. The agency has a right to know."

Peter Jellicoe had been at the Douglaston house this morning, he could have heard me. They had been looking for anything they could use against Matt Jurgens and/or Sarah, and it was just the way Estelle Jellicoe would think and act. It could also be a gaudy lie. If they were all a team, they'd have to lie. I turned to Virginia Garou.

"Have you heard anything from Garou?"

She shook her head, pale, as if afraid to even think about Jack Garou. Ted Garou stood close over her.

"He's a thousand miles away by now," the boy said. "Only when he wants us, he'll find us."

"No," I said, "he's not that far." I told them about El Jazz Latino.

Virginia Garou almost whispered, "That poor woman."

"Ma," Ted Garou said, "I'm scared. He's goin' crazy."

"Sooner or later," she said, "he had to. Always."

I said, "He acted as if he didn't have the fifty thousand Matt Jurgens took home. But if he doesn't have it, how does he know about it? Who told him? Who knew about the money?"

"I . . . I don't know," Virginia Garou stammered.

"Out there in the kitchen," Ted Garou said. "This morning, ma. When Mr. Shaw told us about the money. Jack must have been out there listening a while before he came in."

It sounded like what I'd come to know of Jack Garou. It was an explanation.

"Or," I said, "maybe you two told him long before this morning. Maybe he killed Matt Jurgens, got the money and then lost the money. Or maybe you two killed Jurgens, took the money and still have it."

"Hey, you don't say—" the boy began.

I said, "You were running away from Garou, hiding out at the Grace Hotel, hocking the bracelet for living money. With fifty thousand you could get a long way from Garou and buy a lot of living."

"We didn't murder Mr. Jurgens," Virginia Garou said. "We couldn't have."

"Not for fifty thousand dollars?"

"Not for anything, Mr. Shaw."

"Why?" I said. "Because Ted is really Matt Jurgens's son?"

She got up slowly, eyes fixed on me. Then she began to walk the silent room. There was still the dancer in her walk, and as she talked of the past, I could see her as she must have looked and moved then. "Matt came to New Orleans in 1966. I was working a go-go joint on Bourbon Street. When he came into the place, he looked like any other visiting businessman, his tongue hanging out for the girls and being ripped off with triple-priced beer. But after a while he took out a guitar and started sort of playing along with the band quietlike. You know, when we girls were on breaks, the band just playing background. He came back the next night, and we got to talking. I liked him. I mean, he was sort of happy to be in the club with the musicians and the girls."

Estelle Jellicoe said, "His son? That boy?"

"A guitar?" Peter Jellicoe said. "Musicians?"

Virginia Garou went on walking, her fluid body becoming somehow younger as she talked. "He stayed two weeks, most of it with me. I was married to Jack Garou, had been since I was fourteen, but Jack was in Miami on a big con job that'd take at least a month. Matt played at the club and at a lot of other music clubs I knew then. We were like a couple of kids. The happiest two weeks of my life. Matt even talked of running off together, and that scared me. Jack would find us, I knew that, and I knew what he'd do. I began to get scared that Jack'd come back early. I knew I had to send Matt away. I told him if I ever got free of Garou, I'd come and find him. Before he left, he gave me his business card, told me to call him if I ever needed him. I never did, of course, but I kept the card all these years." She found her handbag, took out a worn business card. We all just looked at it. The agency logo was clear, the word President under Matt Jurgens's name. She looked at it herself, the way a devotee looks at an icon, a talisman.

"When Jack came home, he was on the run and we left town. We lived in Baton Rouge and Mobile, and Ted got born in Memphis. Garou never knew about Matt, thought Ted was his, and I never told him different. It was a long time before we got back to New Orleans. Matt had come back to the club a couple of times, but no one knew where I was. I was thankful for that, I knew what Jack Garou would do to him." She seemed to think for a time about Jack Garou and about Matt Jurgens. Her chest moved in a small sigh. "I never saw Matt again. But one time, a lot later, when Garou had beaten Ted up awful, I told Ted the truth. I wanted him to know that Garou wasn't his father, that someday we'd find his real father and get away from Jack Garou. At least he would, it was too late for me. We used to talk about it all the time wherever Jack took us, whatever scam or violence he got us into. But we never had the chance until he brought us up here for the leukemia con."

She still held the dog-eared business card in her hand. Peter Jellicoe had turned from the window now, was looking at her and at his mother. Estelle Jellicoe seemed to glare at the younger woman and her clutched business card. Ted Garou looked at the floor.

"I had Matt's old card," Virginia Garou went on after a time. "I didn't know if it was still good, and it was only his office anyway. I hoped if I could get to him, he'd at least protect Ted from Jack, but I had to find him. If Jack ever got even a smell of what I was doing, he'd kill me and maybe Ted and Matt, too. So Ted and me ran out and hid in the Grace Hotel. We took some stuff to hock, like a real expensive bracelet Jack swiped down in New Orleans. I called Matt's business number, and he was still there. I mean, some girl told me Mr. Jurgens was still president, I didn't ever talk to Matt myself. It was too many years, you know? I mean, I only wanted to get in touch again for Ted. It's too late for me. I ain't never gonna get away from Jack Garou."

I said, "You found out Matt Jurgens's home address and sent Ted to see him?"

She nodded, smiled at her son. "Ted liked him right off. It was a shock for Matt, I guess. But after he and Ted talked a couple of times, I think he was happy. He didn't have kids, maybe he'd always wanted a son, you know? Anyway, the last time they talked, Matt told Ted he'd help him, take care of him. He said he was going to start a whole new life maybe in Mexico, maybe in South America. He was going to try to live on his guitar, he had a new woman, he wanted Ted to go with him. He said if Ted wanted, I could come along, too, we'd all try to make it together, do what we wanted to do. Only then he got killed, and Jack found us and killed that guy at the hotel, and dragged us back here to finish the leukemia scam."

She went on walking the room for a time after she stopped talking. No one else said anything at first. It was getting dark out now, the sudden dark of a winter night with a storm building to the east out at sea. Ted Garou held his mother's hand. They smiled at each other.

"Damn," Estelle Jellicoe said.

"Why did Garou kill Luis Marquez?" I asked.

"Who?" Virginia Garou said.

"Hearts and flowers!" Estelle Jellicoe said. "What the hell good is all that to Peter and me?"

I said, "The man at the Grace Hotel the night Garou found the two of you."

"He came in with a gun, started askin' me and Ted questions about Matt. Jack goes crazy when he gets attacked, you know? He jumped the guy, took his gun away and shot him with it. We had to get away down the back stairs."

"You think he killed Matt Jurgens, too?"

Ted Garou said, bitter, "He must of followed me."

"And the money?"

They both shook their heads.

"A guitar!" Estelle Jellicoe said. "Hanky-panky on Bourbon Street. My god!"

"Music," Peter Jellicoe said. There was a kind of wonder in his voice.

"Music," I said. "The guitar. That's what he was doing outside the agency all those years. The other part of him, why he didn't do as well on his trips as he should have. He went and played anywhere he could instead of putting time in for the agency. A lot of the time he wasn't even out of town, he was playing his guitar right in the city, staying with a woman named Remedios Marquez. Music, musicians, women who understood his music, that was what Matt Jurgens wanted out of life. A life he couldn't share with Sarah so he hid it until he finally found the reason to make a break. It looks like Ted was the reason, and the fifty thousand was to get started somewhere else. Only he died before he could move, before anyone except Meme Marquez knew he was going to make a move. Unless someone who knew he had taken the fifty thousand guessed what he was going to do.'' I looked at Estelle and Peter Jellicoe. ''You two knew he had the money.''

''But not what he was planning to do with it,'' Estelle Jellicoe said. ''If we'd known, we'd have helped him run. As far as he wanted.''

I looked at the Garous. ''Virginia, did Matt tell you when he was leaving? Or say anything about Jack Garou knowing what was going on?''

''No, I told you I never saw him, Mr. Shaw.''

''What about you, Ted? The night he died?''

''Nothin' about Jack, Mr. Shaw, but he said—''

The silence in the small living room was deep enough to hear the clouds moving outside across the black night sky.

''So,'' I said, ''you were there that night.''

''No,'' Virginia Garou cried. ''He wasn't there that night! He means the night before. A couple of nights before! He—''

''He was there,'' I said. ''I found Ted's footprints on the walk that night. He was out there, and late.''

The boy flushed, he'd made a mistake. ''Mr. Jurgens called me. He wanted to see me, you know? So I went out. He told me he was gonna leave in a couple of days. For Mexico, an' I could go with him. He didn't say nothin' about money. He just said it was gonna be great. I mean, a whole new life for all of us, you know?''

''When did you leave?''

''Around eleven. I remember 'cause the TV was on in the living room, an' the news was just startin', you know?''

Which meant that Matt Jurgens had been alive at 11:00 P.M. If Ted was telling the truth.

"How'd you get home?"

"Long Island Railroad, same as before."

"You walked to the station? In the rain?"

"Mr. Jurgens drove me, you know? I didn't have no coat."

"That's all?" I watched the boy. "You just went home? You did nothing else, saw no one else?"

"I saw someone."

"Who?"

He pointed to Peter Jellicoe. "I saw him."

Peter Jellicoe was standing and looking out the window again as if he wasn't much interested in what was happening in the living room of the semidetached. Now he turned and looked at Ted Garou. "Me? I don't re—"

"That's ridiculous!" Estelle Jellicoe said. "The boy—"

"You're sure, Ted?" I said. "You saw Mr. Jellicoe?"

The boy nodded vigorously. "I knew it was the same guy as soon as we came out of the precinct house an' saw him, Mr. Shaw. He was parked across the street that night in that black Porsche convertible. I'm kind of a car nut, you know? They don't make Porsches like that one no more."

"It was dark and raining, Ted. You're sure he was in the Porsche out there that night?"

"It was him, Mr. Shaw. There's a streetlight across the street, an' the rain was stopped when I saw him. I mean, I know it was him. He was watching the house from the Porsche."

Estelle Jellicoe said, "Don't even talk to them, Peter. The boy's lying and Shaw's fishing."

"No," I said, "I don't think so. Peter almost blurted it out a minute ago, and this morning he accused Sarah of having the fifty thousand. He backed off because Sarah made him realize he would incriminate himself. I mean, suggesting Sarah had the money would mean he had seen her with it, and that would mean he had been out there that night. He didn't want me to know he'd been there, so he backed off the accusation. But he *was* out there that night. The first time we met I had a hunch you both already knew Matt was dead, and the only way you could have known so soon was if Peter or you had been out there.''

Peter Jellicoe walked away from his window into the middle of the room. ''All right, Shaw. I—''

''Peter!'' Estelle Jellicoe cried. ''Be quiet! They can't prove—''

''Damn it all, mother, I'm sick of it! I didn't kill Uncle Matt. I don't want to play this stupid game!''

He glared at his mother. She looked back in disgust. Her whole face was a twisted sneer that said he, Peter, was a weak zero who'd never have the guts to win at anything. He looked away from her, sat down in a shabby armchair, spoke only to the floor and to me.

''I went out there that night to talk to Matt. I was sick and tired of him passing me over, running me down, handing me crap work. I went to have it out: either I got what I was worth, what a family member should get, or I wanted out. If I was going to work at the damned agency, I wanted all the money I could get, and all the power and benefits.'' He breathed hard as if it were still that night, and he was working himself up to be tough.

''What did Matt say?''

Peter shook his head. ''I never saw him.'' He shifted uneasily in the armchair, massive and ineffectual. ''The house was dark except for a light way back in Matt's study and office. I saw someone go around the side of the house so I sat in the car a while. The rain had stopped, and I was going to get out and go in when I heard someone banging things around inside. By then it was getting late so I decided to go home. Only I didn't go home.'' His voice became stronger. ''I drove almost all the way home and all of a sudden felt sick of myself. Damn it, Matt owed me! What was I scared of? So I drove back.''

He half laughed at himself. ''This time I even got all the way to the front door. The house was still all dark and quiet. I was afraid they were already in bed so I went around the house looking for light. A living-room window was open. I looked in and saw light through the open study door. I waited a while under the living-room window. Then Sarah came out of the study. She looked all pale and in shock. She was carrying an attaché case. It was open, and I could see it was full of money! She had it in both hands and went upstairs, swaying and stumbling. I went and looked in the study window.''

From where he sat now in the shabby armchair in Brooklyn, he was still staring into that study. ''It was a wreck: drawers dumped and flung on the floor; furniture knocked over and broken; a lamp smashed. Matt was on his back on the floor beside the desk. There was blood everywhere. Matt didn't move. I could see the knife on the floor. Then Sarah came back. She went down on her knees beside him as if hoping he was still alive or trying to revive him. But I could see he was dead. I was going to go in when she stood up and picked up the telephone kind of slow. I realized she was calling the police so I got out of there.''

''What time was this?''

''Midnight, maybe a couple of minutes after. Back in the car I lighted a cigarette and the dash clock read 12:04. I drove to mother's house to tell her what had happened. As I said earlier, I got there about twelve-thirty. We talked a few minutes, and I drove home. We decided to say nothing to anyone until Sarah told us what had happened.''

Following some kind of inner compulsion Jellicoe took out a cigarette as he finished his story as if somewhere in his mind he was reliving that long night. Estelle had taken his place at the living-room window, looking out, her back stiff with anger and disgust at a son who told the enemy more than he had to. Virginia Garou and Ted sat together on the couch. She quietly patted the boy's shoulder. She seemed uneasy.

''That's the story?'' I said to Peter Jellicoe.

He nodded. ''That's what happened. Sarah does have the money. Or she did that night.''

''And someone killed Matt Jurgens,'' I said.

At the window Estelle Jellicoe made a noise. It was aimed at her son, derisive, to say that she had warned him of what came of saying anything you didn't have to to anyone.

''He was dead when I saw him,'' Peter said.

''And alive when Ted Garou left,'' I said. I turned to the boy and his mother. ''Or was he, Ted?''

''He was! He drove—''

''Never mind, Ted,'' Virginia Garou said. ''I'll—''

At the window Estelle Jellicoe said, ''There's a man in the driveway. He just got out of a blue Datsun, and he has a gun. He also has a woman in front of him.''

I pulled her away from the windows.

''Everyone! Down!''

This time I had my gun ready.

''One of you! Call the police. Now!''

I could see Jack Garou through the glassed-in porch. He was holding his .357 Magnum in one hand and Meme Marquez in the other. The woman held out in front of him, clearly visible in the wide swath of light from the porch across the driveway. He saw me.

The Magnum exploded, shattering glass through the porch. I flattened against the arch between the porch and the living room. Outside, Meme Marquez broke loose and tried for the gray Chevy in the driveway. Jack Garou lunged after her. I got off three quick shots before he vanished with her behind the gray car.

In the rising wind of the coming winter storm I waited.

Eighteen

THE TAUNTING LAUGH came from behind the gray Chevy.

"Close, peeper, but no cigar. Three shots, you should of got me."

Against the door frame I watched the blowing night and the shadows around the gray car. Had Meme Marquez escaped?

"Give it up, Garou!" I called. "The police are coming, and I'll get you if you try to bust in or go for your own car."

"Another miss, peeper," the cool voice said from the night. "Stand up, *chiquita*. Let the man see you."

Meme Marquez stood up out of the shadows. He had her again. His laugh was half amused and pleased with himself and half insane. Meme Marquez stared toward me and the lighted house like a captured spy lost on the far side of no-man's-land. Garou's voice seemed to come from nowhere.

"You see, boy, the way it is I walk when I want to walk."

"Maybe the cops think different."

"Shit, boy, no cop or even the National Guard gonna risk gettin' a spick broad trashed." He laughed again. "Okay, *chica*, down."

He was right. The police couldn't do anything as long
as he had his hostage. There had to be another way.

"What do you want, Garou?"

The unseen menace of his disembodied voice out in the
night seemed to taunt the darkness itself where large drops
of rain had begun to fall.

"Well now, mister, all I wants is what's mine, right?
Now I talked with some nice young lady in blue at the
local pigpen, an' she gimme the word my wife an' boy
was bailed out. Now how about that? Some nice rich folks
they come along an' bail my family out, an' I appreciate
that. Only they ain't with me, you know, so I figured I'd
just come an' get 'em. So what I want is for them to come
on out, an' we'll all be on our way."

From the safety of the doorway arch between the living
room and the porch I searched the night for any sign of
movement. There was nothing. No police yet, no neighbors, no sign of Jack Garou. Only the large raindrops and
the wind.

"I don't think they want to go with you, Garou."

The menace deepened in the unseen voice.

"Don't shit with me, peeper. Where I go they go, an'
I'm going a long damn way this time."

"You're not going anywhere, Garou."

I heard faint movement out in the driveway over the
gusts of wind and rain. My gun was ready. His shout was
harsh.

"Ginny! Punk! Come on out here! You hear me?"

Somewhere far off I heard the quick burst of a siren.
Then nothing. In the doorway I glanced back at Virginia
Garou and the boy. She looked terrified. The boy looked
stubborn.

"They're not coming this time, Garou."

"Shut up, peeper!"

"There's nothing in it for them, not anymore. This time you're going to run right off the earth."

"Ginny!" the unseen voice rose toward a scream. "You're my wife, you understand that, woman? You come on out here!"

Toward a scream, and something else. I heard a rising edge of excitement in the harsh, unseen voice out in the rain. No longer taunting, no longer cold. A deep shiver in the faceless voice, a sudden intensity, a fierce drive as if somewhere out there behind the gray Chevy he gripped his gun harder, his muscles straining.

"You hear me, woman! Leave them other people in there. Leave the damned peeper! You an' the kid come on out right now. I ain't gonna hurt you, girl. I ain't gonna hurt no one if you an' the boy come on out. Not even the peeper."

In the living room Virginia Garou stood up. She smiled down at the boy on the couch, smiled at me. Her eyes weren't smiling.

"It's really just me he wants," she said. "When his voice gets like that. He won't go without me. Even if he did, he'd come back. He'll always come back."

"You're not going out there."

"Maybe he'll let that poor woman go," Virginia Garou said. "He'll kill someone more soon, Mr. Shaw. I can hear it in his voice."

"That's why you don't go out."

Because I heard it, too. A faster breathing under the unseen voice. An excitement. Somewhere out in the night he gripped the gun harder and harder, the blood suffused his face, his eyes were half-closed and shining again with the touch of death.

"We'll go away, Ginny. You an' me. I got our insurance an' our meal ticket right out here. One nice little spick broad they gonna pay good cash money to get back all in one piece. We'll blast all the way out! Blast right out o' this world! Blow 'em away, Ginny! All the shitty pigs an' the rest of the bastards!''

A thickness in his voice, a harsh breathing, and I realized that the excitement was physical, sexual. For Jack Garou killing and the thought of killing was a sex experience, a violent release. For Garou and for other men. The mass murderers and cold killers; the Gary Gilmores and Theodore Bundys and Hillside Stranglers. Certain soldiers: the fifty-year-old elite commando leader and General Patton. Not women. But for some men. For too many men.

"If I got to come in, woman, someone gets dead!"

The menacing voice through the storm, and beyond it I saw them moving. Dark shapes in all the yards across the quiet Brooklyn street, fanning out over the street on either side of the semidetached just out of the line of sight from the driveway. The shine of slickers and weapons through the rain, of gold braid and silver badges. Did they know Garou had a hostage?

Estelle Jellicoe smoked far back against a wall of the living room. I got her attention.

"Did you tell the police he has a hostage?"

"Yes," she said. "They went out. The woman and the boy."

I scanned the room. Virginia and Ted Garou were gone.

"The back way," Peter Jellicoe said.

I ran through to the back door and down the outside stairs to the corner of the driveway. The rain fell in sheets now, blown on the raw wind out of November. I heard the boy's voice arguing with Virginia Garou. I eased to the corner of the house and peered around. Ted Garou and his mother stood in the driveway where it emerged from the shadow of the house. As I watched, Jack Garou rose up from behind the gray Chevy, silent and dripping in the rain like some monster from an ancient swamp.

He motioned them toward him with his pistol. Virginia Garou's voice came low from the night.

"Let her go, Jack."

If Garou answered, I couldn't hear him. I watched them walk to him behind the Chevy. They were between me and him, and there was no way I could try a shot. He kept it that way as he pulled Remedios Marquez to her feet and herded them all back toward his battered blue Datsun behind the Chevy. He knew the police were there.

"I got three now, blue boys! I'm goin' on out, you hear? Later we'll make a deal. I'll be in touch."

He laughed, and as I moved closer, low against the wall of the house along the driveway, he shoved Meme Marquez into the back of the Datsun and turned on Ted Garou.

"Get in, punk."

Suddenly Virginia Garou caught his gun arm.

"Run, Ted!"

Garou flung her away from him and grabbed the boy. Cursing, he shot Virginia and watched her fall in the rain. He held the boy as a shield as the police surged closer, guns out and eager.

"Whoa, blue boys!" Garou laughed. "Back off, you hear? Or I finish the broad an' maybe the kid, too."

He held Ted too close for me to risk a shot from the driveway. If I circled behind the gray Chevy, maybe I could try. I was about to move when the door of the blue Datsun on the side away from Garou opened. Meme Marquez got out of the car. She held a gun in both her small hands. She aimed over the car and shot Jack Garou in the back.

The bullet spun Garou around. Ted fell to the wet grass.

Garou raised his Magnum. Meme Marquez fired again. Garou flung backward, fell on his back on the wet brown lawn. He tried to get up. Meme Marquez walked around the car as the police began to move. She shot Garou again. And again. Until a police sergeant took the gun away from her.

I bent over Jack Garou. Ted Garou and some policemen worked on Virginia. The neighbors were out on all the front steps, in the driveways. Peter and Estelle Jellicoe stood on the steps of the semidetached. Jack Garou lay motionless as I bent down. His lips moved slowly as the rain fell on him.

". . . Aw . . . shit. . . ."

That was all. A police captain with gold braid on his cap stood over me.

"Dead?"

I nodded. Meme Marquez came and stared down at the dead man.

"For Matt and Luis," she said.

"Does it help?" I said.

"A little. It helps a little, mister. For my man and my brother." She turned away from the dead killer lying in the rain. "What I get for falling in love with a gringo."

Nineteen

THE POLICE TOOK US ALL into the precinct. Except Jack
Garou and Virginia. They took Garou to the morgue and
Virginia to the hospital. Ted went with his mother in the
ambulance. They took Estelle and Peter Jellicoe's state-
ments and let them go.

A horde of out-of-precinct police descended on the
South Brooklyn station house. Lew Karnes showed up to
check out the weapons and question Meme Marquez. The
gun she had found in the blue Datsun and used to kill Jack
Garou turned out to be Luis Marquez's missing pistol. It
was the gun that had shot Luis. Lew Karnes rubbed his
hands.

"The fingerprints on the telephone in that Sam Shurk's
room match Garou's, so that closes the books on the Grace
Hotel killings. The owner at that jazz club already fingered
Garou for blasting the clean-up man and shooting him, so
I can wrap it all up. I'll take the Marquez broad and get
her statement."

While Karnes argued with the precinct captain about
that, Rothberg showed up from Central Bunco. He came
to claim Ted and Virginia Garou. He was annoyed that
he'd have to wait until she was out of the hospital. He was

annoyed that Jack Garou had escaped him. Lieutenant Guevara sent a man from Douglaston to check out on Matt Jurgens.

"I guess Garou found out that the kid was really this Jurgens guy's kid, and about that money too," the Douglaston cop decided. "Tried to blackmail Jurgens maybe. Whatever, this Jurgens made some mistake, and Garou killed him."

They finished with me about 10:00 P.M. I got my car and drove to the hospital. Virginia Garou was still in serious condition but was stable and resting comfortably—whatever that meant for a woman with a .357 Magnum hole in her shoulder. They said I could talk to her if she was awake. Ted Garou was sitting small and alone in a straight chair outside her room. He looked up at me as I came along the silent antiseptic corridor.

"She's gonna be okay, Mr. Shaw." He smiled, but his eyes were still frightened.

"Let's go in and talk to her."

"We can?" He blinked those scared eyes at me, puzzled and suspicious. I nodded.

"Jack?" he said. "He's dead?"

"He's dead."

"Then why—?"

"Come on," I said.

Virginia Garou lay in the high white bed in the hushed late-night hospital, pale and looking younger than her hard years. I imagined how she had looked to Matt Jurgens when he walked into that New Orleans go-go club with his guitar. How she must have looked when she listened to his playing, accepted him as he had wanted to be.

"Mr. Shaw," she said. "You don't think it's over?"

Her eyes were open, watching me, and I knew she had heard all we had said in the corridor as if she had been lying there waiting for me, knowing I would come to the hospital.

"I don't think Garou killed Matt Jurgens."

She said nothing, motioned to Ted to come to the bed close to her. Small, he stood only a head higher than she was where she lay in the high bed.

"It's not his style," I said. "He had his gun."

Ted said, "But he got to have, Mr. Shaw! He followed me out there. He blackmailed Mr. Jurgens, an' then Mr. Jurgens wouldn't pay an' Jack killed him! I mean, maybe Mr. Jurgens tried to use that knife an' Jack took it away an' killed him like he did with that Luis Marquez an' his gun!"

I shook my head. "He never acted as if he knew you were Matt's son, and I don't think he knew Matt had that money until I told you two about it. He was looking for who had it in El Jazz Latino."

"Jack got to of killed him for that money!" Ted insisted.

"How?" I said. "He didn't even find you two in the Grace Hotel until after Matt Jurgens was dead. How could he have known about Matt Jurgens?"

In the small room, its other two beds empty, we were as isolated as voyagers on an alien planet. Even the distant footfalls on the hard floor of the corridor were remote, unreal in the silence of the unseen hospital outside.

"Then," Virginia Garou said, "who did kill Matt Jurgens?"

I faced Ted. "You said you left the Douglaston house at eleven that night. Matt drove you to the railroad station because it was raining. You took the train home."

"I did!"

"You said you saw Peter Jellicoe parked across the street. You could see him easily because the rain had stopped. How could it have been raining and not raining? No, you blew your own story. You saw Jellicoe, yes, but later, *after* it had stopped raining. You left the house at eleven, it was raining, Matt drove you to the station. But you went back after it had stopped raining, and you saw Peter Jellicoe when you left the second time.''

The faceless silence of the hospital filled the small room. The distant sounds of machines and slow voices, breathing and soothing, the clink of metal and shuffle of soft feet.

''You think Ted killed him?'' Virginia Garou said. ''Why?''

''It could have been you two who were blackmailing him,'' I said. ''You could have wanted the fifty thousand to help you get away from Garou. Perhaps Matt denied he was Ted's father, was going to call the police. Matt did try to use that knife, but it was Ted who took it away from him.''

''A boy Ted's size?'' Virginia said. Her voice was low and weak but steady now. ''No, Mr. Shaw, and there is no motive. Jack's big con is over, and so is my little one. Ted isn't Matt Jurgens's son, we had no hold on Matt, no reason to kill him.''

The boy watched her, half-ready to laugh, waiting to be told she was joking.

''Matt came to New Orleans in sixty-six,'' she said, speaking slowly, carefully, ''only we didn't have an affair. Matt was only interested in playing his guitar. One day we talked some, I told him about the dream I had of going to New York to get in shows, and he gave me his business card and told me to call him if I ever did get to New York. That's all, just a nice guy. I mean, I still liked Jack then even though I was scared of him, too.''

''But, ma,'' Ted Garou said. ''Jack wasn't my old man!''

"I'm sorry, Ted," she said. "Garou never wanted kids. We was married nine years before Ted was born. Jack beat him, used us both for his scams, dragged us from hole to hole. Always on the run, always brutal. Drunk and mean most of the time. Using us in his rotten schemes. You ever live all your life with a mistake you made when you was fourteen? You ever see your kid scared all the time? Sick and hungry and scared? And Jack would never let us go. I had to give Ted something to hang onto. Something to hope for, you know? A future, an escape, a dream, I guess. A secret life when it got too bad with Jack. So I told him about Matt. Said I'd been in love with Matt Jurgens, and Ted was his son. I had the business card, I invented the rest. Matt Jurgens was a nice, decent man, and one day we'd find him again, and we'd get away from Jack Garou. Sometimes I even got to believing it myself."

Ted had walked slowly away from the bed and was sitting now on a straight chair against the wall. His head was down. He'd believed what his mother had told him.

"Ted believed Matt was his father," I said. "He still wants to."

"I know," she said, looking toward the boy but letting him handle it himself for now, "and I'm sorry, but he had to have his hope all those years. Now he doesn't need it anymore. He's old enough, and Jack Garou's dead." She turned her head carefully to look at me. "And Matt knew he wasn't Ted's father. So when we ran out on Jack, and Ted went to find Matt, I called Matt first and told him the whole story. It's funny, he really remembered me. He'd often wondered what had happened to me. He said he wouldn't tell Ted, he'd play along, and he'd even try to help us really get away from Jack. The last couple of times he talked to Ted about Mexico, and I even thought for a minute it might work. Then Jack found us."

"So you had no motive to kill Matt Jurgens, no reason for blackmail."

"None, Mr. Shaw."

"But Ted did go back to the house that night."

The boy was still sitting staring at the floor, looking at nothing. He had lost two fathers and an illusion in the same night.

"I went back," he said, almost toneless. "When Mr. Jurgens left me at the station, I found out I'd lost the pawn ticket on the bracelet, so I had to walk back to the house." He brushed at his eyes as if there had been too many losses too fast. Or perhaps he was remembering that night as it had really been. "The place was pretty dark, but I saw some light still on back in Mr. Jurgens's office so I rang the bell. I rang a lot, but no one came, you know? I went around an' looked in some windows. The TV was still goin' in the living room, only no one was in there. So I looked in the office, an' Mr. Jurgens was lying there next to his desk on his back. There was blood all over, an' Mrs. Jurgens was sittin' in a chair sort of rocking an' rocking, you know? I mean, she just rocked in the chair, an' her eyes was all big an' blank like a blind guy."

"In shock?"

"I guess. I mean, I guess I was in kind of shock, too. I mean, that office was just like I'd left it maybe half 'n hour ago, an' Mr. Jurgens was dead! He was my real father, an' he was gonna help us get away from Jack Garou, an' he was dead! Nothing'd changed an' everything'd changed."

"The office was just as you'd left it? No mess?"

"I could of still been sittin' right there, Mr. Shaw."

"What did you do?"

"I got out of there. I was scared. It'd stopped rainin',"

an' when I got out front I saw that Peter Jellicoe in his Porsche across the street.''

"What time was this, Ted?"

"Aroun' eleven-thirty. I mean, the news was just endin' on the TV in the living room. I couldn't hear it so good through the window, but some comedian come on and I remember thinkin' he was up there bein' funny, an' there wasn't no one to hear him.''

"Then what?"

"I walked to the station an' took the train to the city. Next day Jack found us at the Grace an' made us go back on the scam with him."

As he finished, he finally looked up from the floor. There was an emptiness in his young eyes, but somehow the frightened look was gone. They seemed older, his eyes. Maybe they were. From the bed Virginia held her hand out to him in the dim light of the bare hospital room with its empty beds like ghosts or a past that was gone. He went to stand near her again. She looked at me.

"Ted had no reason to hurt Matt, Mr. Shaw, and neither did I. If Jack didn't find out about Matt and kill him, I don't know who did."

"I do," I said. At the door, going out, I stopped. "You're free of both now, Garou and the illusion. You can have a real life. No more con games. You'll have to answer for the scam in Brooklyn, but I think they'll go light. I'll tell them all about Garou."

"Thank you, Mr. Shaw," Virginia Garou said.

They weren't bad people. They had just needed a dream to make their life better, an escape from reality. Most us need that at some time.

Twenty

THE HOUSE WAS all dark, but I knew she was there. I rang. There was no answer. The front door was unlocked. I closed it behind me and saw the glow of the cigarette across the living room.

"Why the dark?" I said.

The cigarette glowed, faded. "Estelle called. She told me all the good news about that man Garou. She said he killed Matt and everyone. She was surprised you hadn't called to tell me."

She sat in the same chair she had the night Matt died when we talked in the half-light after the police had gone. Alone in the house then and now. I walked to her.

"So," she said, smoked, "I knew you'd come here."

I watched her vague shape behind the red point of light that waxed and waned in the silent house like a beacon light that moved closer and farther away. "Sarah—"

"Not yet. I've waited ever since the night Matt died. I've been alone, Paul. I don't want to be alone tonight."

"Sarah, I can't—"

"Yes, you can. You're a man not a boy. Just tonight."

She stood up in the darkness. My eyes were accustomed

now, and as she bent to stub out her cigarette, I saw the outline of her naked body under a thin robe.

She walked into the hall and up the stairs. Through the silence I heard the soft creak of a large bed, the rustle of cloth against smooth skin. I went up the stairs.

Afterward I reached down to my suit-jacket pocket for a cigarette. Whenever I've tried to quit, it's always this cigarette that defeats me. Afterward, lying beside a woman, pure and isolated in another world, timeless.

"When did you know?"

I said, "Not until tonight, really. It was always possible. From the first. But I didn't really know until tonight."

"Possible, yes," she said. "What proof?"

Somewhere out in the still-blowing storm a solitary man walked the empty suburban street. "The call that night. If Matt was still alive, you were wasting critical time. You're too smart not to know about paramedics. The call was to hide the time of death, imply it had just happened. An attack by some outsider, and Matt was still alive. There was no fight, but he had a rip in his shirt—the kind a man might get if his wife grabs his arm in an argument, and he pulls away. No fight, but stabbed more than once, a kind of fury. A thief, a transient, a blackmailer, when they kill it's one shot and run. There was nothing wet, not even the inner sill at the open window. Meaning it hadn't been open very long when I got there."

Naked in the dark of the big bed she smoked and looked toward the windows with their squares of ghostly light from the single street lamp below.

"The window didn't have to have been open long if Matt was alive when I called you. The rest is all guessing, Paul."

"There's the money," I said. "You didn't kill him for

it. I doubt if you knew he had it here. But you found it and took it. You were alone here, Sarah. No one else.''

She smoked. ''I took the money. I heard the noise down here, came down, found him stabbed, called you. You told me to call the police. While I waited, I saw this attaché case on the floor in the mess and opened it, and there was all that money. I knew I was going to need money. If the police found it, they'd take it as evidence, and I needed it. I was wrong, I know that, but I wasn't thinking clearly that night, I was confused so I took the money. But I didn't kill Matt. I called you because I was confused. I couldn't think. I was all alone. . . .''

She faded off in the dark of the bedroom where she had slept with Matt Jurgens. She was working it all out for the jury, preparing her story, practicing. Another con game. She was listening to her own voice, judging the effect, the impact.

''It won't work,'' I said. ''Peter Jellicoe was here that night, waiting outside to see Matt. He got here about eleven-thirty, heard noise, so drove off. But he came back. The front door was closed so he walked around the house looking in. The living-room window was open, he saw you with the money. He looked in the office window and saw Matt dead on the floor. The office was a wreck, just the way we found it. He saw you come back and pick up the telephone. He thought you were calling the police, left quickly. But you were calling me, setting me up.''

Naked in the dark, she smoked. ''Paul, I didn't want to tell you, but that boy *was* here that night. I saw him, heard him talking with Matt. He must have—''

''So you did see Ted Garou,'' I said. ''You knew he was here; I think you knew Matt drove him to the station. What you don't know is that he came back about eleven-thirty. The front door was closed and no one answered his rings. Maybe you were in too much shock then to hear the doorbell, or maybe you heard and just sat and hoped whoever it was would go away. But Ted Garou didn't just go away again; he wanted that pawn ticket, so he walked around the house, too. The window was closed. He looked into the office. He saw Matt on the floor. He saw blood. He saw you rocking in a chair. He saw the knife on the floor, and he saw that nothing had been touched in the office—no drawers out or dumped, no furniture smashed, no files opened, no mess at all.''

This time she said nothing. I heard a car stop outside. I listened. Slow footsteps walked back and forth in the night. A man walking a dog? Someone not ready to go into his house?

''Ted Garou was here at eleven-thirty that night,'' I said. ''Matt was dead; there was no mess in the office at all. Peter was here at midnight. Matt was still on the floor, but by then the office was wrecked. There was no outsider, you heard no fight. You killed Matt, then you opened the window and wrecked the office to make it look as if there had been an outsider in the house. You called me to confuse action and time and maybe get some help. I don't expect you meant to kill him. I think you overheard him and Ted Garou, heard that Ted was his son, and that he was going to Mexico with the boy and Meme Marquez. I think you argued, he told you it was true, and you grabbed the knife and killed him.''

She moved beside me on the bed, her soft breasts swinging shadowy in the darkness silvered by the light from the solitary street lamp below. She stubbed out her cigarette, lit another. Her hands were steady, and her voice was low and quiet.

''He was going to be a musician. With some woman I'd never known about. All those trips. A musician, that's what he wanted to be. A guitar player. I'd wasted my life. And he had a son. He was going to leave me. He didn't want a divorce. He didn't care about a divorce. A divorce would be traumatic, hurt me. He didn't want anything from our life: not the agency, not the house, the stocks or bonds or savings. He would take just enough money from the agency to get a good start in a new life; I could have everything else. His new woman didn't care about a divorce or any of that. All he really wanted was to leave me and our life. The only reason he came after me the day I went to you the first time was that it was too soon; he wasn't ready to tell me yet! He wanted a quick, clean break. From me! He was leaving me to play the guitar in Mexico with a bastard son and a woman named Marquez! I saw the knife on the desk. I stabbed him. I . . . I must have gone crazy. It was him bringing that boy into the house. It made me go crazy.''

I got up from the bed, began to dress in the dark bedroom.

''It turns out the boy isn't Matt's son after all. Just a kind of escape story the mother gave the boy. Matt knew but didn't want to hurt the boy so didn't tell him.''

She made no move to get up or to stop me from dressing. I had no worries about her doing anything. She had killed Matt Jurgens in a moment of blind rage. She was too smart to complicate it.

''Peter can run the agency for a time,'' she said.

''He won't thank you. He doesn't really like agency work, but he'll do what Estelle tells him to do.''

''Weak,'' she said. ''Like Matt. All those years letting me make him live a life he didn't want to. Then just running away. He never wanted to hurt me. Too weak to realize that nothing could hurt me more than saying he never wanted any of our life, had hated it all! He cared so little he didn't even want a divorce, as if I didn't even exist. I could keep everything; all our years made no difference to his real life at all.'' She seemed to think about all that in the dark bedroom. ''Well, Peter won't have to run the agency for very long, I hope. I can afford a really good lawyer. I was out of my mind, wasn't I? That boy and all. The shock. A little luck, a good lawyer, and it shouldn't go too badly for me.''

I walked to the door.

''Paul? Thanks for tonight. Be nice in court.''

The last I saw of Sarah Jurgens was the small red glow of her cigarette in the dark bedroom.

The storm still blew on the late-night street. A black car sat at the curb. Lieutenant Guevara walked up and down hunched against the wind, his hat dripping rain.

''Get it all?'' he said.

I took the miniature tape recorder out of the coat pocket where I had my cigarettes. A small con on Sarah. ''It's all there, but you probably can't use it in court.''

''It gives us an edge. With the testimony from you, Ted Garou and Peter Jellicoe, we should be able to get a plea out of her lawyer. Murder two, maybe, but probably manslaughter; her lawyer'll be a good one.''

''A deal?''

Guevara looked at the house and the street. ''We don't send rich Anglos to the chair, Shaw, and not many to jail for very long. Not unless it's a real far-out first degree, and not then if they got real money. This wasn't even close to murder one. Murder two at the worst, so with a good lawyer she'll take a plea to manslaughter with a light slap. Be back running her business in a couple of years.''

''Too bad it wasn't Garou all the way.''

''Him we'd have fried and been proud of it.''

I left him looking at the dark house on the quiet suburban street. It wouldn't even get to court, and maybe that was the biggest scam. I drove to the parkway and opened up my little red Ferrari in the small hours of the morning. I needed Maureen. Maybe I'd just drive straight on past the city and across the whole wide land to Arizona.